"You're human."

Craig moved closer to her before continuing, "I know that somewhere underneath that polish, there is a warm, human woman trying to get out."

Fay stepped back quickly, furious with herself and with him. "You simply can't resist plumbing the depths to see what you might find, can you? You seem to think you have a magic key, an open sesame to what goes on under my skin."

His voice roughened. "Tell me, Fay, is there something wrong with warm, human women? Is it a weakness in your book to have ordinary human emotions?"

"Of course not," she snapped. "I just prefer to keep them to myself, and—"

"Until a moment like that happens," he murmured, "which, by definition, has to be shared. And then you can't help yourself."

Angry beyond speech, Fay glared at him. But he was right, damn it!

KATE KINGSTON was born in Yorkshire. She is married, has one daughter and two grandchildren and now lives in the Nottingham area—famous for Sherwood Forest! Her interests include walking, embroidery and travel. The idea of writing always beckoned, but Kate feels that it was her meeting with a perfect stranger, who predicted that one day she would be a writer, that fired her with the enthusiasm to actually go out and do it.

Books by Kate Kingston

HARLEQUIN ROMANCE

14—BITTER INHERITANCE
2981—ALIEN MOONLIGHT

KATE KINGSTON

wild champagne

Harlequin Books

TORONTO • NEW YORK • LONDON
AMSTERDAM • PARIS • SYDNEY • HAMBURG
STOCKHOLM • ATHENS • TOKYO • MILAN

Harlequin Presents first edition January 1992
ISBN 0-373-11428-1

Original hardcover edition published in 1990
by Mills & Boon Limited

WILD CHAMPAGNE

Printed in U.S.A.

CHAPTER ONE

FAY stood in the rain, her mass of chestnut hair spangled with bright beads of dampness. She stared up at the red brick walls of her inheritance and tried to feel happy.

During the brief flight from Paris to Gatwick this morning she had caught sight of her horoscope in a discarded newspaper. 'Contradictory influences colour your day,' she had read. And now, as she stood on the weedy crescent of gravel, her mouth twitched wryly: the astrologist seemed to have got it right.

In Paris, soft sunshine had bathed the rue de la Paix where she and Christophe had sat over morning coffee before he drove her to the airport. But now that scene seemed light years away from the dripping Sussex lanes and the rain-battered rhododendrons in the gardens of Brantye. And whereas coffee with Christophe had been relaxed and pleasant, lunch with Mr Seymour, her late grandfather's solicitor, had seemed stiff and chilly. Fay gathered that he had been a close friend of her grandfather, and she had inferred that, beneath his formal good manners, he disapproved of her. Still, that couldn't be helped, she thought rebelliously, and, after all, I didn't ask Grandfather to leave me this—this depressing, run-down old pile. And after that old family quarrel it never even occurred to me that I would be mentioned in his will. However, here it was—a big, neglected house which probably needed a fortune spending on it . . .

She sighed; then, squaring slim shoulders under her wide pink tweed scarf, she selected the right key from the bunch she had been given, inserted it into the lock and found to her surprise that the door swung open immediately. And straight away she was precipitated into a flood of memories, fifteen years old and even older, of days when her mother was still alive and the old house had been bright with the freedom of summer holidays.

Now the hushed gloom of the place seemed to reach out, dankly, to absorb her. Now there was only a sad silence.

She swallowed an unexpected lump in her throat. It belongs to the past, she reminded herself sharply. Those memories belong to childhood, to the days before Mother died, to the time before Claudia came upon the scene, and Father and Grandfather quarrelled so bitterly. So there was absolutely no point in getting nostalgic about the place. Heavens above, what on earth would she do in a house of this size, not to mention the expense of its upkeep? Apart from that, her life was in Paris. So Brantye would have to be sold, and coming back here for a last look at it was nothing more than a whim, a sentimental journey.

A faint noise made her start suddenly and spin round. A door leading from the gallery above her had opened, and a man stood there looking down at her. Her heart gave an involuntary thump of alarm, and she took a step backwards, her grey eyes narrowing. 'Who are you?' she said sharply.

He didn't answer immediately, just walked unhurriedly to the top of the broad staircase, then came slowly down—almost, Fay thought, as if she weren't there, as if she hadn't spoken. Her irritation mounted as he approached, watching her with a dark, aloof gaze. He must be about six feet two—or more, she decided, forcing herself to return his scrutiny bravely despite a prickle of fear in her chest. There was a craggy strength in his features, an arrogance in the line of his nose and the black, lowering eyebrows above fathomless, lustrous eyes. The shadows of the dim hall accentuated the hard jawline and resolute cleft of his chin.

She took another step back towards the door, noting the breadth of shoulder and strong, deep chest revealed by his open russet suede jacket.

When he spoke, his voice, though quiet, had an authoritative resonance, and for no reason that she could think of a responsive awareness flickered through her.

'I'm Craig Mackenzie,' he answered at last, coolly, as if her question had been an impertinence. 'And I take it that you're Rafaelle Armitage.'

Fay's eyes widened in surprise, then she nodded shortly. 'That almost sounds as if you were expecting me,' she remarked. She forced herself to look away from the dark eyes which had compelled her gaze. 'So it appears that you have the advantage over me, Mr Mackenzie. *I* expected to find the house empty.'

'Well, we're not *quite* strangers,' he said offhandedly.

For a moment Fay stared at him, puzzled; surely if they *had* met before she would have remembered him?

'I'm sorry,' she said carelessly at last, 'I don't remember the occasion... But why are you here now? I wasn't aware that anyone else had the keys to Brantye.'

He leaned one elbow on a carved oak buffet, apparently in no hurry to answer, and Fay's irritation increased. 'Legally speaking,' she added, 'I should warn you that you're trespassing.'

Heavens above, how pompous she must sound! But his self-possession infuriated her. By rights he should apologise, or at least make some attempt to explain his presence. And there was surely no getting away from the fact that Craig Mackenzie, whoever he was, had no legal right to be wandering through the house—*her* house.

The grimness of his mouth relaxed momentarily. 'Then, if we're asserting our legal rights, Miss Armitage, perhaps I should point out that you're—dripping on *my* carpet.'

'Your——?' Fay looked down, then her face cleared. Suddenly conscious of her damp state, the rain-flecked shoulders and rain-misted hair, she faced him again. 'Ah, I think I understand... You mean that the contents of the house have been left to *you*? Mr Seymour did mention that the house only had passed to me, but I hadn't quite——'

'Taken it all in?' His eyes narrowed, and there was no mistaking the sudden chill in his tone. 'No, I'm sure your inheritance must have come as quite a windfall. After all, you had been out of touch with your grandfather, hadn't you? Fifteen years or so, isn't it?'

Fay's face lit with sudden heat. He despises me! she thought with mingled amazement and anger. He sees me as some kind of vulture, in at the kill for a feast. She bit back the retort that sprang to her lips and said in tight, controlled tones, 'As I remarked previously, Mr Mackenzie, you have the advantage; you seem to know quite a lot about my affairs.'

'Oh, not a lot,' he dismissed carelessly. 'But enough. You didn't attend Julius's—your grandfather's—funeral, did you?' The words condemned her.

For a moment Fay glared at him. Who the hell was he to take up this attitude of censorship? She moved forward, tilting her chin and pushing away the hair which had begun to curl damply on her forehead. She wasn't cold now, but warming with an anger lit, incredibly, by a man who, so far as she was concerned, was a total stranger. 'I do think I'm beginning to understand,' she murmured cuttingly. 'I recognised the same note of disapproval—although more successfully disguised—in Mr

Seymour's voice only a couple of hours ago. Well, I owe you no explanations, Mr Mackenzie; I don't even know who you are or how you fit in—apart from the fact that you've inherited the contents of the house. But just for the record, let me tell you that I wasn't even aware of my grandfather's death. It happened while I was in Rome on business,' she went on tartly. 'I got back to my Paris apartment to find Mr Seymour's letter giving me the news. And by that time the funeral was over. So, now that I've enlightened you, perhaps you would return the compliment?' When he didn't answer, she added, 'Or maybe you prefer to prolong the mystery?'

'Not if it bothers you,' he murmured. 'And it seems to.' He moved easily away to stand by the window looking out on to the puddled gravel drive and Fay's hired car. 'I've told you my name. You also know that your grandfather—Julius—left me——' he gestured vaguely '—the contents of Brantye. As for the rest, my remembering you—I saw you briefly fifteen years ago, the last time you were here, in fact. But possibly you didn't see me.' He turned then to face her. 'As I recall it, yours was a very short visit. And after you had left, with your father and his new wife, old Julius was devastated.'

Fay bit her lip. 'What a good memory you have for the unpleasant details,' she remarked scratchily. This man's knowledge of her personal circumstances was an intrusion into her privacy. 'What were you doing here at the time?' she asked. 'Working?'

Craig allowed himself a wintry smile. 'No, I was a guest, *almost* family, you might say. If you must have an explanation, you need to know that my father was the son of Julius's second wife by her first husband. You knew, of course, that your grandfather had married twice?' When Fay nodded, he went on, '*Your* father was his son by his *first* wife. So it almost makes us related, in a loose kind of way. Well? Does that satisfy your curiosity?'

Fay shrugged, flicking the fringed end of her scarf negligently over her shoulder and making a gracefully dismissive gesture. 'It answers my question,' she said indifferently. Then her tone hardened. 'You do realise, I hope, that I shall almost certainly sell this house, so perhaps you would arrange for your furniture to be taken out as soon as possible.' She paused, then turned towards the door. 'I'll come back tomorrow. No doubt by then you'll have finished taking your inventory—or whatever it was you were doing when I arrived. And I'm sure you'll have no objections if I look around privately then.'

'Leaving so soon? Going—where?'

Fay's eyes widened, her clear brows arching haughtily. 'If it's of any interest to you, Mr Mackenzie, I shall make for Haywards Heath and find a hotel somewhere. Goodbye. I don't expect we'll meet again.'

She opened the door, and heavy though it was she was almost flung back against the wall as a gust of wind tore the handle from her grasp.

'It would be very foolish to go anywhere in this storm,' he murmured, watching her expression with a glimmer of amusement.

Fay stared out. The wind had risen alarmingly, tormenting the branches of the beeches with a sound like surf breaking, and scattering the rooks.

'I don't think I have any alternative,' she snapped. Obviously this man bore an enormous prejudice against her. Hadn't he implied that she had neglected her grandfather? No doubt he bitterly resented the fact that she had inherited Brantye. But what did it matter? Let him think what he liked! And yet it rankled that he was so ready to apportion the blame so unfairly in the matter of an old family quarrel which, surely, was none of his business, and for which she couldn't be held responsible. It was adults' business. Forget it, she told herself sharply. In a couple of days you'll be back in Paris, and Brantye will be in the hands of an estate agent.

She pulled the scarf more closely around her, then glanced up as Craig said, 'Of course you have an alternative. Behind you there are ten bedrooms,' he went on crisply. 'Just think—all of them yours! Take your choice.'

Fay watched him speculatively for a moment. 'Thank you for reminding me, Mr Mackenzie,' she said quietly. 'And is it *your* intention, too, to spend the night here because of the storm?'

He laughed suddenly, the movement of his firmly sculpted mouth lending his jaw an even more pronounced strength. 'Now that sounds as if it has the makings of a very interesting situation,' he drawled. The humour was echoed in his eyes, a reflected light. To Fay they looked almost black, but surely that wasn't possible? Yet there was very little difference in colour between pupil and iris. His strong hair curled thickly above a broad forehead, framing his temples and curving into his nape, lending a noble line to the silhouette of his head against the grey light of the window behind. 'That isn't an invitation, is it, Fay?' He paused as she stared, her heart suddenly bumping erratically. 'It *is* Fay, I believe?' he went on softly. 'I don't seem to recollect anyone here ever mentioning you by your full Christian name.'

His use of the diminutive had brought the warm blood surging into her face, and his utter self-command exasperated her. 'No, it is *not* an invitation,' she snapped. 'Definitely not.'

'Oh. Pity. So you propose to throw me out into the teeth of this gale?' The thought seemed to increase his amusement, and as the green flecks in Fay's eyes sparked angrily he purred, 'Oh, come, Fay. Surely if I'm sufficiently generous to offer you the use of one of *my* beds for the night, you would be charitable enough to allow me the use of one of *your* rooms?'

Suddenly the utter absurdity of the situation struck Fay. Trust Grandfather to put me on the spot, she thought resignedly. He was always an awkward, unpredictable old man.

'Shall we forget it?' she said wearily. 'Sleep where you like, Mr Mackenzie. Feel free to use any of—*my* rooms. I'm going, storm or no. Just make sure that you're away early tomorrow morning, will you? And please lock up when you leave—that is if you value your furniture. I understand that this area is very attractive to burglars. Goodbye.'

She ran down the two shallow steps and got into the car. Craig Mackenzie had put the finishing touches to a difficult day.

Originally, Fay had planned to leave Brantye for London where she would spend a day or so with her younger sister, Vicky. That, at least, would have salvaged something pleasant from this day. Fay recalled with affectionate indulgence the untidy flat off the Fulham Road which was Vicky's idea of the right ambience for an actress just setting out on a career which would, hopefully, one day spell her name in lights. However, finding Craig Mackenzie at Brantye had ruined Fay's intention to take a last look around the old place, alone. So going to London tonight was out of the question—and doubly so, she decided, noting the rising intensity of the storm as she turned the ignition key.

Beyond the iron gates the lane was almost awash, and the noise of the wind in the trees had increased alarmingly. So it had to be Haywards Heath or somewhere even nearer. The shorter the journey, the better, in these conditions.

Damn Craig Mackenzie. If it weren't for him she might have lit a fire and changed. Then while her clothes were drying she could have wandered through the house, privately and at leisure, indulging this crazy nostalgia for scenes that were almost forgotten. And perhaps there would be some tinned food still in the house; on a more practical note she realised that she was hungry. French breakfasts weren't exactly sustaining, and she had merely toyed with a salad during the uncomfortable lunch with the solicitor.

She gave the ignition key another twist, and the starter coughed, stuttered, then died. She tried again, more gently. There was a series of jarring, protesting noises, but the engine didn't fire. Damn! This certainly was not her day! 'Come on, oh, come *on*,' she moaned, and tried again. It was no use.

A shadow fell across the car window, and she looked up to see Craig Mackenzie holding an ancient black umbrella and grinning down at her. He opened the car door. 'Trouble?' he asked creamily. 'It's all this rain, I expect. Well, the offer of a bed for the night still stands, you know.'

'Oh, I don't think——' she began quickly. She bit off her words as the wind rose to a sudden roar, and after a moment gave a resigned shrug. 'It seems that I've no alternative,' she muttered.

'I'll take your things.' He reached into the back and pulled out her small suitcase. 'And red roses, too! How *did* you guess? They're my favourite flower!'

Fay shot him a withering look. 'If we're being facetious,' she said acidly, 'I recognised your affinity with their thorns.'

Christophe had bought the roses for her at the airport. It was the kind of courtesy that came as naturally to him as breathing.

Craig laughed softly, infuriatingly. 'But these have no thorns,' he murmured. 'Or hadn't you noticed? No, probably not. I'm sure that red roses and such romantic trappings are commonplace in your life.'

Fay narrowed her eyes and set her small chin firmly. 'Look,' she began heatedly, 'I don't know——'

'Let's get inside,' he interrupted brusquely as the wind blew a great douche of rain into their faces. 'Here, you take the umbrella.'

His hand cupped her elbow masterfully, half lifting her up the steps, his touch unleashing a sudden power that raced through her like hot mercury. Instinctively she recoiled, bowing her head down and away from him so that he wouldn't see her face, for she sensed that such a raw and totally irrational reaction must show.

'The central heating's off, of course,' he remarked, apparently oblivious to the effect of his touch upon her, 'but I lit a fire in the housekeeper's room.'

'Providential,' she said faintly, walking ahead of him through the hall, and fighting an absurd desire to run. It was utterly beyond comprehension that he could have aroused such a sizzling response in her, especially after their earlier acrimony, and all she wanted was to keep as far away from him as possible.

Inside the snug little room which Fay vaguely remembered, she took off her scarf and shook it. Although from the back her figure was boyish, slim-hipped, long-legged and almost sexlessly rangy, showing off to advantage the catsuits and harem trousers she often wore, the high thrust of her small breasts and the neat cinch of her waist were entirely feminine, and her movements as the droplets of water hissed on the hearth revealed for a moment the fluid curves beneath her raspberry-pink wool dress.

Craig had put down her case and was straightening. For the merest fraction of a second he froze. 'Well, well,' he said softly, 'you've done a lot of growing up in the fifteen years since I last saw you.'

Fay glanced at him sharply, blushing. 'Who hasn't?' she retorted. 'And now perhaps you'll go away and let me change in privacy.'

'Of course, if you're sure I can't be of any further help,' he purred.

'Quite, quite sure.' She closed her door firmly behind him, breathed a sigh of relief, and vigorously pulled the dress over her head. From her case she took out a moss-green sweater with a bulky, cowled neck—she had past experience of the draughts in Vicky's flat and had come prepared—stepped into matching trousers, then bundled up her hair into a casual knot on the top of her head. The dress and scarf she draped over a chair by the fire and saw them begin to steam gently.

What an unsatisfactory predicament to find herself in, stuck here for heaven knew how long! She wanted to be free of Brantye and its sad, damp atmosphere. Free, too, of Craig Mackenzie, who seemed to have got under her skin like a splinter. She stared idly around at the ink-stained round table where Mrs Manners used to do her household accounts, at the gloomy, dark red wallpaper, shivered, then went into the cavernous kitchen. A search through the store cupboards revealed only a jar of lentils and some damp salt. The chill of the stone-flagged floor struck upwards through her velvet mules, and she shivered again.

A sharply poignant wave of homesickness hit her for the efficiency of her bright grey and yellow tiled kitchen in the apartment off the Boulevard-St-Michel, her comfortable sitting-room with its view of crooked red roofs, the colours and bustle of the Paris markets, the scent of Gauloise cigarettes . . . And Christophe, her link with normal, pleasant, predictable living . . . She had a sudden need for his stability.

When she went through into the hall Craig was stacking photograph albums into boxes. She armoured herself against the disturbing black glance he flicked over her. 'I'd like to ring Paris,' she said crisply. 'That is, if the phone hasn't been disconnected?'

'No, it hasn't. You can make your call from the morning-room. You *do* remember where that is?'

'Vaguely.' She gave him a wide-eyed, innocent stare. 'But I'm working on it,' and she went out.

She dialled Christophe's number with fingers eager to reach out and touch someone familiar, *safe*, ending the strange sense of disorientation which seemed to have grown as the afternoon wore on. And as she waited for his secretary to put her through, she leaned against the wall, her eyes closed, not wanting to be reminded of other days spent in this room.

'I've such a lot to tell you,' she began when he came on the line, 'the crux of it being that Grandfather has left me his house.'

'But that is splendid!' Christophe's comforting voice came through the static.

Fay laughed. Christophe was under the impression that he could sound almost English at times. At this moment the trait seemed very endearing.

'You mightn't say that if you saw it,' she told him.

'I can't hear you very well. Where are you calling from? Your sister's?'

'No, there's a violent storm here, so I decided not to go up to London today. I'm at the house now.'

'Alone?'

Fay hesitated for only a moment before she said, 'Yes.' Explaining Craig's presence was too complicated. 'I just wanted to tell you that I'm about to put your roses in water. I didn't thank you properly this morning; I was in such a hurry... But thank you, anyway.'

There was a burst of static, then Christophe saying, '...will be back soon?'

Fay laughed. 'Of course! My work is in Paris. And my home——'

'And I, too.' Christophe chuckled.

'Yes.' Fay gave a satisfied smile. 'Of course you are. I'd better go now. Take care.'

'You, too, *chérie*.'

She replaced the receiver, noticing that she hadn't completely closed the door between the hall and the morning-room. So no doubt Craig Mackenzie had heard every word. Well, so what? Carelessly she sauntered through. How on earth was she going to spend the evening? Certainly not in conversation with *him*! And she had no intention of aggravating this crazy, threatening sense of nostalgia by offering to help him sort through his possessions. She would find a book somewhere, and go to bed early.

Heavens, but she was hungry! She had worked late last night and had fallen into bed, too tired to eat, her mind still centred on the designs for next spring's collection. The trouble with fashion, she reflected, was that you looked so far ahead that the here-and-now became less important. But a slight, and rather embarrassing, rumble in her stomach indicated that it was! She glanced covertly at Craig, hoping that he hadn't noticed.

Presumably he had a car somewhere around the place, maybe tucked away in one of the outhouses where it would have remained dry. She would just have to swallow her pride and ask him to lend it to her. There must be a pub or restaurant not too far away——

His voice broke into her thoughts as if he had read them. 'I don't know about you, but I'm ready for something to eat. There's a decent enough place along the road which stays open. Join me?' His tone was laconic, uncaring.

'Is that an invitation?'

He eyed her speculatively for a long moment, and she forced herself to return his gaze coolly. Then he shrugged. 'Please yourself, of course. But if you choose not to accept, then you're going to feel pretty hollow by tomorrow morning. There's nothing in the house.'

'I know. I looked. And I appreciate your concern for me,' she added silkily.

'Oh, I'm not really concerned.' His eyes flicked over her rather disparagingly, she thought. 'I'm quite sure you can look after yourself very well. But I want to eat, and if you do, too, then we might as well do it together.'

Fay's lips twisted for a moment, then she began to laugh.

He stared at her enquiringly. 'What's so funny? Did I say something?'

Fay shook her head. The twist of hair, caught and knotted carelessly on her crown, tumbled to fall in a thick rope, curving on to her shoulder and framing one side of her face. She saw Craig tense momentarily.

'Well?' he gritted, after a moment. 'If there's a joke, do tell.'

Fay made a little moue, shrugging. 'Oh, it's not funny, really, I suppose. But—all this...' She stared around. 'A decaying old house which brings back memories, and which I don't want... And you—so blatantly disapproving of me, and the fact that I've inherited it... And our being thrown together like this, and the wretched storm to prolong the agony... And now we're going to dine together.' She paused, then went on thoughtfully, 'I remember that Grandfather had a liking for playing tricks on people. As a child I found some of them rather...unkind, uncomfortable. Suddenly I get the feeling that he must be helpless with laughter now.'

There was no answering smile on Craig's face. It was sombre, closed against her. He got up abruptly. 'There's an assortment of wellingtons in the vestibule off the hall, just in case you don't remember. And an array of oilskins and anoraks, too. I'm sure you'll find something suitable. My car's gone to be serviced, so I'm afraid we'll have to walk. Think you're up to it?' Again, the disturbing, black glance skimmed over her, its expression telling her nothing. 'It's about half a mile.'

'I dare say I could manage that,' Fay returned.

Her face was beginning to burn again. He really does dislike me, she thought. Apparently *he* saw no humour in a situation which had thrust them, willy-nilly, into each other's company; if he could have managed even a smile it might have thawed an atmosphere which had suddenly iced up again. But obviously he thought her assessment of the situation frivolous. And there was also something in his manner that condemned her as the kind of woman who expected special treatment. Well, she knew the score: she expected *nothing* from him, she stormed inwardly, fiercely resenting his ability to make her feel small and silly. What on earth's the matter with me? she asked herself, as she thrust her arms into a blue oilskin jacket. How is it that he has a positive talent for making me feel—edgy, suddenly insecure?

She had difficulty in keeping up with his long strides as he hurried her along, his hand gripping her upper arm firmly. She opened her mouth to protest that she felt as if she were being taken into custody, but the wind snatched away her breath as they butted their way down the lane. And she was relieved when they reached The Feathers and she could disengage her arm, which still stung from his touch.

He brought her a dry sherry as they waited for their steaks to be cooked, and during the meal she limited her conversation to monosyllables.

But by the time coffee was served Fay felt much calmer. Oddly, the day's irritations had all but disappeared. The warmth of the small, oak-panelled room seemed to lap her in an ageless, comforting security. After all, the worst was over now, she thought. Tomorrow she would be with Vicky, and perhaps the following day she would return to Paris... Paris, and Christophe, and the busy, safe, pleasant life she was forging for herself. Surreptitiously she glanced at her watch. At half-past eight perhaps she could plead tiredness, and they would leave. Hadn't Craig made it clear that he, too, was not exactly enchanted by present company?

He saw her movement and said smoothly, 'Not in a hurry, are you? Another phone call to make, perhaps? If so, you can make it from here.' His unfathomable eyes seemed to weigh her as if she were some uncertain commodity.

She felt herself flush and sat back. 'No particular hurry,' she said pleasantly, glancing around her. But after a moment she crumpled her napkin and put it on the table beside her empty cup.

'Good,' he said, ignoring the obvious hint, 'because I enjoy lingering after a meal. Don't you? And besides,' he added, 'I'm addicted to coffee.' He straightened, caught the eye of the waitress and gestured smilingly towards their cups. Obligingly she came across to pour refills. 'Do you see much of your stepmother?' His tone seemed idle, without any obvious curiosity, as he took a cheroot from his pocket, looked enquiringly at Fay, then lit it as she nodded.

But his question had thrown her violently. She felt her spine go rigid as her eyebrows flew together. 'Claudia?' she asked sharply. 'No. No, I don't. She lives in Cannes,' she added.

He rested his chin on his hand. An attractive hand, Fay realised distractedly, with long, fine fingers but in no way delicate or effeminate. Like his face, they held an illusion of lean strength. 'Oh, but surely Cannes isn't a million miles from Paris?'

Ten million miles away, Fay thought bitterly, and that's not far enough. 'Claudia and I were never very close,' she murmured stiffly.

'Oh?' For a split second a flicker of surprise lit his eyes. As he drew an ashtray towards him he said thoughtfully, 'The last time I saw you—the *only* time until today—I was lying in a hammock slung under the trees at Brantye. I was there convalescing after a road accident. Julius had told me to make myself scarce during your father's afternoon visit. I remember that you and Claudia came out into the garden with the dogs and played with them. You seemed very close to her then.'

Fay widened her eyes, propping her elbows on the table and watching him coldly above interlaced fingers. 'Do you know something?' she said icily. 'I get the distinct impression that you have a computer printout on me and my affairs.'

'Nothing of the kind,' he drawled. 'Why on earth should I? But I'm as observant as the next man, and it's just a picture that has stayed with me, that's all—a green lawn, black Labradors and the two of you laughing together in the sunshine.'

'Well,' Fay said abruptly, 'we didn't laugh together for long.'

She glanced at him, reading accusation in his gaze. Her feeling of relaxed ease dissolved. One way and another, Craig Mackenzie had a very low opinion of her. So maybe it was time she put things straight, although the reason why she should worry about his views eluded her.

Carefully suppressing any defensive note in her voice, she stirred her coffee and said baldly, not looking at him, 'When my mother died, the spring went out of my father's step. It's a cliché, I know, but that's how it really was. A man of thirty-seven, prematurely old, apathetic, slow... It seemed that, not only had Vicky and I lost our mother, we'd lost our father, too. Then Claudia came along. Transformation. She seemed to give him back his—*life*, I suppose.' Fay looked up then, expecting to see cynicism written large across those saturnine features, but there was only a concentrated attention that made it much easier to continue.

'Claudia was about twenty-two at the time. And I adored her for what she did for Father. She—restored him, you see.' Fay took a sip of coffee. 'Of course,' she resumed thoughtfully, 'she couldn't replace Mother... But I was—adrift, trying to find a focus for all the feelings a girl has for her mother. I needed a friend, a mentor. Also Claudia was young enough for there to be some empathy between us. And she was very, very lovely.' Fay gave a taut, painful smile. 'It's so easy—at least, it was then—for a ten-year-old girl to fasten her love on a woman who had the kind of beauty that Claudia had. At least, that's how it was at first...'

After a moment Craig nodded, then said, 'But it didn't last?'

Fay blinked. 'None of it.' Her voice grew hard. 'Not my feelings for her, and certainly not hers for me and Vicky—that is, if affection had, indeed, existed. But, most important, her feelings for my father——' She stopped. She had said enough without going into the distressful scenes of the following years. And after all, Craig Mackenzie, despite the family connections, was a virtual stranger. 'And,' she continued, in a matter-of-fact tone, 'that day when you saw us would be the only time that Claudia ever came to Brantye. It was her introduction to Grandfather. Perhaps he saw something in her that we were blind to at the time... But it was too late; she and my father were already married.' Fay paused for a while, then went on, 'And later that same afternoon, Grandfather made his feelings about the marriage abundantly clear. My father was incensed on Claudia's behalf. We made a hurried exit. And that was the last time any of us saw my grandfather,' she concluded flatly.

'It's a pity though that your father didn't make his peace with Julius later,' Craig said idly, watching Fay through a thin skein of blue smoke.

Fay sighed. 'Oh, Claudia wanted him to, but my father felt that she had been insulted. And, despite everything, he still doted on her,' Fay added sadly. 'But perhaps, in time, he would have come round to the idea and attempted to mend the rift. He died—very suddenly,' she added shortly, moving restlessly on the high-backed settle. Even now, five years after her father's death, she couldn't speak of it without feelings of self-reproach and guilt. If she hadn't been so determined to take those photographs of wild flowers, to be used in an art project she was working on, her father would never have fallen to his death.

Craig's voice pulled a shutter over her reflections, as he said, 'You must have had quite a tough time, one way and another.'

Fay glanced quickly at him. Did she detect a note of sympathy in his voice? Then she almost laughed aloud. Sympathy? From him? He was merely being polite, making the obvious remark.

'Tough? Oh, I don't know...' she said coolly. 'After all, we did have a few fun months together—the four of us—before I realised that the rot was setting in.' She shrugged. 'Then Vicky and I were sent away to school. And, of course, in the circumstances there could be no more holidays at Brantye.'

'Didn't it ever occur to you—after you grew up, I mean—that your Grandfather might like to see you?'

There it was again! The veiled rebuke in the quiet conversational tone. 'Why *should* he have wanted to see me?' Fay argued. 'As I understood it, he was through with my family.' She hesitated, then continued in a softer manner, 'Occasionally though, more recently, I *did* think of coming back to see him, of just walking in out of the blue... But I remembered him as a rather daunting old man. All that wild white hair... Quietly caustic, or bellowing so that his voice seemed to fill the house. He wasn't like other people's grandfathers. And anyway,' she went on dispiritedly, 'I could anticipate his welcome only too well. Remarks about the prodigal granddaughter and the fatted calf and so forth. You may not know this, but I was always a great disappointment to him because I wasn't a boy.' She smiled painfully. 'So, you see, I was under a handicap. And when Vicky was born he wouldn't even see her; it took him about three months to come round to the idea that he had yet *an-*

other granddaughter.' Her mouth twisted into a regretful curve. 'And now, it's too late.' She drank the last of her coffee and put her cup down. 'So he has heaped coals of fire on my head by leaving me his wretched house. I wish I knew why.'

'Because you're the elder of the only two Armitages left, of course,' Craig said. 'And the name has always counted for something in these parts.'

'Perhaps.' Fay shrugged. 'Still,' she added bluntly, 'you've got the furniture, and that should fetch quite a healthy sum.'

For a moment Craig stiffened, his eyes snapping with black fire. 'You don't seriously think I'm jealous of your inheritance, do you?' he clipped out. 'That I resent your getting the house?'

Fay met fire with ice. 'Well, don't you?' There had to be some reason for his instant dislike of her, and this seemed to be the most obvious one.

'Certainly not,' he snapped. 'I wasn't related by blood to Julius, and I had no expectations.'

'All the same, it sounds as if you were closer to him than anyone else,' Fay retorted shrewdly.

'And whose fault was that?'

'Not—mine.' She was surprised to feel herself trembling in a passion of dislike. What on earth had prompted her to confide in him?

She stared at him, her grey eyes rebellious, and for a moment the atmosphere crackled with tension like a gathering storm, needing only a further word from either of them to break into violence. Beneath the table she clenched her fists. Oh, what wouldn't she give to get up and walk out? She must have been mad, rerunning old memories with their laughter and tears, love, disillusionment. It had needed only that one idle question about her stepmother to unleash the emotions she had relegated to the past. How satisfying it would have been to know that her car was outside, and that she could go away and forget that Craig Mackenzie, with his prejudice and censure, ever existed. He's all the 'A's, she thought angrily—arrogant, autocratic, and totally antipathetic. And devastatingly attractive? a tiny voice inside her head suggested.

But he seemed insensitive to her rage. He drew on his cheroot and said, 'Tell me about your Paris.' Then he added with a glint of humour, 'Sorry this place isn't exactly the Taillevent, but it was the best I could come up with at such short notice.'

With an effort Fay gave a small, polite smile. 'Oh, I'm very grateful. I was extremely hungry. Mr Seymour didn't think much of me, *either*. It rather inhibited my appetite at lunchtime. And I'm quite sure that an account of *my* Paris would bore you,' she added sweetly.

She didn't intend opening her heart any more to Craig Mackenzie. His insight into her connections with England was enough. Her life in Paris was something else, not to be shared with a disapproving stranger into whose company she had been unavoidably thrust.

Her career as chief knitwear designer for a fashion house had been carefully hewn out of talent, hard work and a little luck. Not to mention a resolve to put the past behind and start a completely new life, relying only upon herself. She had decorated her apartment with quiet flair; her few good pieces of furniture had been bought after periods of resolute scrimping and saving. Paris, with its sights and sounds and smells, was her life, present and future, and she did not intend holding it up for Craig's censorious scrutiny. So she reverted to his earlier remark. 'You say that you hadn't expected Grandfather to leave you anything,' she remarked idly, 'but I gather you must have been his greatest friend. It seems rather an unlikely alliance.'

For a moment Craig's face was an arrangement of sharply defined shadows. Then he said quietly, 'He was very good to me. I owe him what I am now.'

'Really?' Fay murmured in awed sarcasm. 'And what, exactly, *are* you now?' Heavens, she thought, this man wins all the prizes for sheer arrogance.

He regarded her coldly in silence, the expression in his eyes a rebuke. She stared back defensively, unwilling to drop her gaze in subjection, and then, oddly, quite unable to. A ripple of strange excitement ran through her, seeming to suspend all other reactions to him, as she realised that she was holding her breath.

She moved again restlessly as he said, 'Julius had a wide knowledge of art, painting. You, of course, may not have been aware of that. He encouraged my own interest, moulded and directed it.'

'Oh? The Svengali touch?' Fay said brightly, trying to flatten the excitement that still fluttered inside. 'So you're an artist?' Well, she thought, appearances could certainly be deceptive!

'My living depends on *other* artists,' he corrected. 'I'm what is commonly described, rather euphemistically, as an expert. And,' he went on, as if divining her thoughts, 'that is the general term, so don't accuse me of arrogance.' He smiled slyly as she bit her lip and looked away. 'I tend to specialise in the pre-Raphaelites. And I think that says it all.'

'With admirable clarity,' Fay agreed.

'Oh, I could go on,' he said blandly, 'but you're looking at your watch again. Strange, though, my interest being the pre-Raphaelites and your name being Rafaelle, wouldn't you say?'

'Oh, I don't know,' she demurred. 'If you look hard enough you can see coincidences everywhere. And you wouldn't find *me* a very rewarding field for specialisation as I'm sure you realise only too well. Look, I'm really rather tired——'

'Not to mention bored,' he interrupted. 'Still, we have managed to kill a couple of hours. And at least the *steak* was enjoyable,' he said, with such significant emphasis that she wanted to hit him. He got up, carelessly shrugging into his waxed jacket and politely holding out her oilskin.

Outside the wind was dying and the sky clearing to allow a few pricks of starlight. This time he didn't take her arm as they walked, and she was thankful for that. She planned to get away first thing the following morning and stop for breakfast at the first pull-in she saw. She hoped that the car would start, but if not then she could telephone for help.

Brantye seemed more forbidding than ever as they went in. Quickly he switched on lights and closed curtains, but Fay shivered, thrusting her hands deep into her pockets.

'There used to be flowers everywhere,' she said suddenly, her voice catching. 'And those two Labradors always lay on the sunlit patch near that chest... And it was warm, always so warm...'

She had been thinking aloud, and now she realised that Craig was watching her, half smiling. She felt vaguely apprehensive. Perhaps the pub would have had a room for her; if she had thought about it earlier she could have asked. She didn't relish the idea of spending the night alone in this gloomy old house with its conflicting associations. But she wouldn't be alone, would she?

As if Craig could read her mind, he said smoothly, 'You don't *still* begrudge me the use of one of your rooms, do you?'

'No,' she answered, 'providing I may have the use of one of your beds.'

She slipped off her jacket and chafed her cold hands. 'What an inheritance,' she murmured defeatedly. 'Obviously it ought to mean a lot to an Armitage, but really, what on earth can I do except sell it?' She was speaking half to herself, troubled by a strange sense of betrayal. 'It needs—oh, people, voices...' She pivoted slowly, looking at the looming seventeenth-century furniture, the great, soot-stained fireplace yawning like a black mouth, and shuddered. 'Spooky.'

'Well, then, we'll find you the brightest bedroom,' Craig said bracingly. 'At least you'll be warm. The blanket chests are well stocked.'

Fay chose one of the smaller rooms at the eastern end of the gallery. 'And where,' she asked, swallowing nervously, 'will *you* be sleeping?' She put down a pile of sheets.

'At the opposite end of the gallery,' he murmured lightly. 'Where else? And don't be afraid, I'm not in the habit of paying nocturnal visits, if that's what's worrying you!'

She spun around, her chin high. 'Worrying me? Are you crazy? I'm not afraid; I'm not that kind of girl.'

He nodded, his eyebrows lifting sardonically. 'No, of course you're not.' He made the words sound almost like an insult. 'Sleep well.'

CHAPTER TWO

FAY slept badly, troubled by confused, unpleasant dreams, and awakened to sunshine streaming through the faded curtains. She dressed quickly, anxious to be on her way, and when she went downstairs there was no sign of Craig. She was surprised to find that her relief was tinged with a sneaking sense of loss.

The wine they had drunk with their meal on the previous evening had left her with a dry mouth, and there was nothing here so cheering as a cup of tea. She put down her case and found a thick glass in one of the kitchen cupboards. She was taking the first cold sip of water when Craig came in, carrying a box.

'Breakfast,' he said casually, answering her startled expression.

'You mean—you've been shopping *already*?'

'No. I collected this lot from home.'

'Oh . . .?' Fay's eyebrows rose a little higher. 'Are you saying that you live—*locally*?'

'Didn't I tell you?' he said smoothly. 'I live at The Lodge. I bought the place when Harvey and his wife left. You remember Bill Harvey, the gardener? That was just after Julius went into the nursing home; the staff were retired and the house shut up.' Craig wasn't looking at her; he was taking out bread, eggs and a coffee percolator.

Fay stared, her grey eyes bewildered. 'You live at The Lodge—only a stone's throw from here . . . Yet you slept *here* last night!'

He turned then, straightening up, a glint of amusement dancing in his eyes. In the thin morning sunlight she could see the first steel-silver hairs at his temples. 'Not for any ulterior motive, if that's what you're wondering,' he said softly.

Fay blinked and drew herself up. 'Mr Mackenzie——' she protested heatedly.

'Oh, *come*,' he interrupted. 'Surely, with our having spent the night together, you can relax so far as to call me Craig?'

She ignored the interruption. 'You completely mistake my meaning,' she said with attempted dignity. 'I'm not so vain as to suspect every man I meet of the desire to—to——'

'Take you to bed?' he finished. Those remarkable eyes slid over her, and she felt her body's instinctive response beat a wave of warmth into her face. 'Well,' he said thoughtfully, 'it might be a good thing if you weren't quite so trusting. Luckily it was I whom you had for company.'

'Luckily? That's a matter of opinion,' she said caustically, needled by his complacent tone. 'So what made you decide not to go home for the night?'

'Simple. You didn't seem too happy to be in this place, and I guessed that——'

'I'd have been even less happy knowing that I was alone?' Fay bit her lip, looking away from him and wishing that she didn't have to be grateful to him for this consideration. 'But didn't I tell you that I wasn't the kind of girl who frightens easily?' she said lamely.

He laughed. Suddenly he seemed more human, more approachable. 'You did make it fairly obvious that you had no fear of a mere *man*,' he agreed. 'But you seemed to have other fears, fancies... Didn't you?'

'Yes,' she admitted after a moment. 'You're quite right. I'd have loathed being alone in this—this mausoleum. Well,' she went on with a little laugh, 'I hope you slept well in a strange bed. And—thank you, Craig.'

He was still watching her with a flicker of wry amusement, as if he realised how difficult she was finding it to express her gratitude. 'Oh,' he said carelessly, 'just part of the Mackenzie service. And I expect you'll be wanting to get away, so shall we start with grapefruit? I'll do it. I'm used to fending for myself. You can lay the table. Cutlery in that drawer.'

She was pleased to have a mundane, everyday task to occupy her, although with Craig so close there seemed nothing mundane about this morning, she thought, with an uneasy pang. As he moved about, the clarity of the morning light lent a sharp purity to every feature of that strong face, so vivid that the air around him seemed to be charged with an indefinable, disrupting force that searched her out with laser-beam accuracy. She began to wish that she had got away before he came back to the house. And now there was no escape, and it irritated her that she should feel so subjective to his magnetism.

There was an electric toaster plugged in above the battered pine dresser, and she reached for the bread knife a fraction of a second before he did. As her fingers closed around the handle they were immediately covered by his hand. His touch scalded. All the disturbing forces which she had sensed and tried to reject were suddenly centred in the palm that held her hand captive, pinioning her, so that for a moment she was paralysed. A great bubble of breath rose inside her, but before it could come out as a gasp she turned her head away, her whole body stiffening against him.

Then, magically, she was able to free her hand. She rummaged blindly in a drawer, not daring to look at him in case she revealed this unbelievable, maddening vulnerability to whatever power it was he had over her. And, most of all, she didn't want to read his expression; that, no doubt, would be one of amusement at his effect upon her. Particularly after her cool assertions about men.

Heavens above, she told herself disjointedly, it was only a *touch*. But a touch that had unleashed incredible responses inside her. And she didn't want them! Her life was safely mapped out, the operative word being 'safe'. There had been too much agony and confusion in the past. Too much betrayal: the painful uncertainties of life with Claudia, the sight of her father's unhappiness, even as he remained devoted, and not least her own feelings of overwhelming guilt after he died. She had once been the plaything of her own emotions. But not any more. Over the past few years she had made her life—and herself—as secure as possible. And something warned her that with Craig Mackenzie all that could be threatened.

'I think,' Fay murmured distractedly, after an everlasting silence, 'I ought to ring Vicky just to make sure she realises that I'll be coming up to town today...' She dropped the soup spoon she was clutching and escaped. She forced herself to walk calmly into the hall, concentrating her gaze on the dust motes that danced in the morning sunbeams. But the feeling of panic still rocked her. If, an inner voice insisted, she could be so receptive to Craig's merest accidental touch, what might it be like to find herself in his arms? Or, supposing that controlled yet sensuously modelled mouth were laid against her own? She shivered, then caught herself up savagely, clenching her stomach muscles and biting down hard on her lower lip. However, such conjecture was futile, thank heaven; the opportunity to learn the answers would never arise.

Her fingers still felt limp, almost fluid, as she dialled Vicky's London number, and a moment later her sister's breathy, familiar voice drew her back to reality.

'Weren't you really supposed to be coming up last night?' Vicky asked vaguely. 'I mean, I wasn't sure... But anyway, with that awful storm going on I guessed you would stay put.'

'I figured you would think that, so I didn't bother ringing.'

'That's OK,' Vicky said, and Fay smiled. Vicky's attitude to life was in complete contrast to her own. Vicky was vague, untidy, and paid scant attention to anything as restrictive as watertight arrangements. Sometimes she turned up at Fay's Paris flat without even a phone call to say that she was coming. 'I just felt like the trip,' she would say airily. To her, that was explanation enough. Her will-o'-the-wisp personality refused to be pinned down by convention—a quality which Fay often envied but couldn't imitate. 'But anyway,' Vicky was saying, 'it's a good thing you've caught me now. Guess what? I'm going up to Manchester to audition for a theatre group. Isn't that great? Wish me luck.'

'Of *course* I do,' Fay said warmly. She laughed, infected by Vicky's excitement. 'Lots of it. When will you be back?'

'Tomorrow, I think. When are you going back to Paris?'

'Well, it should have been tomorrow, but——'

'You're not going without seeing me first,' Vicky protested.

'No, of course not. Look, I'll come up to town today as planned——'

'And stay the night at my place? Fine. Nick, the guy in the next flat, will let you in. I'll be with you tomorrow.'

'All right. So I'll leave on Monday instead.'

'Great. Oh, just one thing... Seen anything of Claudia recently?' Vicky's voice had steadied on a note of thoughtful speculation.

'No.' Fay was surprised. How odd that Claudia's name should crop up twice within twelve hours. 'Why do you ask? She's in Cannes as far as I know, or floating around on the fringes of *la dolce vita*.'

'She isn't, you know. She turned up here a couple of days ago. Said something about being on her way to Worthing for a wedding. But, well—Grandfather left me some money, and perhaps I'm being uncharitable to connect that with Claudia's visit... Anyway, she mentioned you, so I ought to warn you that I got the distinct impression that she's wanting to see you.'

'I can't imagine why,' Fay said shortly.

Vicky laughed. 'Don't be naïve, darling! You've got Brantye, haven't you? And it's not a lot of use to you, but it's got to be worth a few nice round figures. Look, I must fly. Nick's giving me a lift to the station, and he's honking like crazy outside. I'll tell you more when I see you. And keep your fingers crossed for me.'

Absently Fay replaced the receiver and made her way back to the kitchen. It was almost two years since she had seen Claudia. And Vicky's suspicions could just be right. But it wasn't only Claudia's avarice that rang warning bells in Fay's head; it was the memory of Claudia's knack of—of spoiling things. As she had tried to do between Fay and her father... She had even fanned the flames of that last quarrel, which Fay would have given anything to forget.

They had been on holiday in the Pyrenees, Fay rather resentful at not being allowed to go to Florence with a group from the art college, but Claudia had been unwell. Exactly what was wrong had never been specified. To please her father, Fay had spent much of the time fetching and carrying for Claudia. Then, one day, her unhappiness had spilled over. Claudia had retired in tears, complaining of selfish, ungrateful stepdaughters, refusing to be comforted by her bewildered husband.

'Well,' he had said ruefully, later, coming out of Claudia's room to see Fay's tear-stained misery, 'there's no sense in the two of you moping. Come on, we'll go and photograph those wild flowers you're always talking about...' Tears stung Fay's eyes now as she remembered the details of that last day with her father. The climb, the beauty, the resurgence of that old sense of companionship, then the horror...

And then, much later, Claudia had spoiled things between Fay and Pierre, her first French boyfriend. That particular love-affair hadn't had a chance once Claudia had arrived on the scene in Paris...

'Everything all right?' Craig was looking at her enquiringly and Fay blinked, snapping back to the present. Well, she consoled herself, at least Vicky's unwelcome news had brought her out of the dangerous trance induced by Craig's touch.

'Fine,' she said, sitting down at the furthest end of the table, and picking up her grapefruit spoon. 'At least... Well, I was hoping to see Vicky today, but she's going to Manchester to audition for a part in a play. She's an actress, you know.'

'Yes, I do know,' Craig said calmly.

Fay glanced up, her expression wary. 'It *still* amazes me to learn just how much you know about my family, she murmured.

'It's all quite simple, really. I met Vicky at Julius's funeral. Didn't I tell you?' Then he added, 'I was pleased to find that at least one of the Armitage sisters cared enough to attend.'

'Now just a minute,' Fay began hotly, 'I've explained why I wasn't there, and I don't——'

'Yes, I heard you.' He threw away the words dismissively. 'And it seems that you don't have a very close relationship with Vicky either, or you would have known that she came.'

Fay laid down her spoon in a sudden flare of anger. Perhaps now was the moment to get up and walk out. But she couldn't give him the satisfaction of knowing that his opinion of her mattered that much. Speaking in a carefully level voice, she said, 'I sense an implied criticism there. *Yet again.* And it seems to be quite a habit you're acquiring, taking me to task about my relationships with my own family.'

'Flicked you on the raw, did I?' he said with grim humour. 'Although I would say it was less of a criticism than a mere passing observation. What a sensitive lady you are.'

Fay let go a small sigh of barely concealed exasperation. 'And now let me surprise *you*,' she said. 'Just for the record, Vicky and I *are* close, but we don't live in each other's pockets. I don't keep tabs on her, nor would she want me to. The fact that I accept that she has to live her own life without too much interference from her elder sister is one of the reasons why we have a good relationship. Or can't you understand that? To you, is love—possession?'

He didn't answer, merely watched her over the rim of his coffee-cup so that she couldn't see his mouth, only those remarkable eyes, darkly impenetrable between thick lashes.

'And,' Fay went on with heavy patience, 'as Vicky and I had time only for the briefest of conversations before she dashed off to the station, the funeral wasn't even mentioned. But no doubt I'll hear all about it tomorrow. And now, if you've *finished*,' she added, stressing the word in double-edged implication, 'I'll clear away.' That should put him firmly in his place, she thought.

But the irritation he had provoked in her the previous afternoon was reinforced by this added evidence of his determination to think the worst of her. Who was he, she stormed inwardly, to pass judgement on her relationships with other people? Just what business was it of his?

'So what are you going to do today?' he said suddenly.

Fay got up, raking long fingers through her hair and shrugging. 'Go up to town, I suppose,' she answered coldly. 'I'll take in an exhibition, perhaps. See a film. I don't know.'

'On such a lovely day? What a waste.' He leaned back, lifting his arms to lace his fingers behind his head, and tilting his chair backwards. The movement accentuated the breadth of his chest and shoulders, and Fay concentrated on the crockery she was holding.

'And I suppose *you* have a better suggestion,' she retorted, then wished she hadn't spoken as he grinned at her disarmingly.

'Oh, lots,' he said, and laughed. 'But perhaps they should remain unspoken.'

'That's what I like,' Fay said acidly. 'Good, constructive ideas.'

He lowered his arms, letting the chair settle again as he idly turned over his empty eggshell. 'I see. It's something constructive you want, is it? Well, how about *not* going up to town? Instead I'll give you a trip down Memory Lane. Then you can renew your acquaintance with all your old haunts around here. That is, of course, if you haven't moved too far away from your beginnings.' His glance ran over her, warming as dark rum, from the slight dusting of freckles that lent an odd, gamine youthfulness to her patrician features, to the designer-label sweater with its cowl that framed her slender neck, down to the perfectly cut trousers with their intricate seaming.

'The answer—to all your questions—is: I don't think so. but thank you all the same,' she added sweetly after a moment.

'Well, it's up to you, of course,' he said carelessly. 'I was merely trying to be constructive.' He got up with a lazy grace that drew Fay's glance. 'It probably wasn't much of an offer to a girl who clearly has little time or inclination for sentiment or nostalgia. And,' he went on, his voice spiking suddenly, 'before you accuse me of further criticism, that, too, was merely an idle observation.'

'You're *so* perceptive,' Fay said quickly. 'I expect your work must help to sharpen your eye for detail.'

'Could be,' he said indolently. 'Still, maybe I'm quite wrong. Your refusal could hint at something else.'

'Like what?' Fay looked up sharply.

His eyes met hers, boldly, challenging. 'Fear?' he offered softly.

Fay attempted a derisory laugh. 'Fear of what, I wonder? I'm getting rather tired of your speculations about me. What have I to be afraid of, for heaven's sake?' She snatched up the plates and turned towards the sink.

'Do you really need *me* to spell it out?' he purred. 'Oh, come, Fay. You're an intelligent lady.'

'Spell *what* out? I really don't know what you're talking about.' She ran the tap noisily, her head bent so that her hair screened her hot face, while she groped for something trite to say which would lead her out of the emotional quicksands she seemed to be treading. But her confusion went so deep that she couldn't produce anything. Craig's nearness threatened her on all fronts; the faintest whiff of Paco Rabanne cologne reached her, coupled with an almost lost scent of heather from his tweed suit.

She went back to the table again, keeping well away from him and reaching for the toast rack. But as she lifted it his hand fell on hers. The sensation was there again. Electric! He was right, damn him. She *was* afraid. The rack clattered on the table and she cursed her own vulnerability.

'Afraid of the *past*,' he said softly.

Chagrined, she stared up at him. Part of her felt relief that he was unaware of the potency of his touch. But another deeper side protested: was it possible that so strong a sensation as she had felt—that shattering thrum that still vibrated inside her—was confined only to herself? But apparently it was, for Craig was going on, 'You can't wait to get away, can you? Old memories—even tender ones, or should I say *especially* tender ones?—have no place in your life. So you write them off, together with the people they concern.'

Fay was still trying to bring herself under control, unwilling to accept that the touch of a man so unlikeable could exercise such power. She moistened nerveless lips and whispered, 'You're so clever. How *did* you acquire such insight? And why bother to try and psychoanalyse my attitudes? Or perhaps you're an authority on women and our poor little frailties,' she added, her voice firming in scorn.

'Not an authority,' he answered smoothly. 'Rather call it—discernment.'

Heaven forbid, Fay thought wretchedly, that he should discern the annihilating effect of his hand closing over hers!

'Well, you're totally wrong about me,' she snapped.

'Am I?' His eyes studied her frankly for a moment, a glint of speculation in their depths, daring, taunting, almost jeering.

'Certainly.' She flung down the dish mop and turned to dry her hands. 'All right, then. I accept your offer!' As she hung up the towel she wondered desolately why it was so important to prove his theory wrong. Did it *really* matter if he thought her a heartless bitch?

'Fine,' he approved. 'We'll drive around, find somewhere for lunch, then afterwards you can come back here, pick up your car—it's all right now, by the way—and drive off into the sunset. You've nothing to lose but a fairly aimless day in London.'

Haven't I? Fay questioned silently, dismayed by her own recklessness. She hardly recognised herself. And what, exactly, had gone into this man, that he could throw her so, by word and by touch? And now, out of stupid pride, she had committed herself to spending the day with him! She must be mad! What had happened to the cool, clear-headed person she thought she was?

'So that's settled,' he went on, when she didn't speak. 'The garage will be delivering my car in half an hour or so. Meanwhile I'll dump all this stuff back at The Lodge.' Capably he stowed butter and marmalade and the remains of the loaf into the carton. 'Don't go away, will you?' He looked up suddenly, catching her gaze.

'Why should I?' she said coolly.

'Oh, I don't know... Something in your eyes, perhaps. A kind of trapped look.'

'You're being utterly ridiculous. Good heavens, it would take more than a day out in the country to trap *me*.'

'Thanks for the information. Not that trapping ladies is in my line, exactly.'

'I'm glad to hear it,' she retorted.

While he was gone she managed to regain her composure. Self-assured, arrogant... oh, yes, Craig Mackenzie was those, all right! And so completely confident of his power to analyse her motives accurately. Maybe, with some girls, that would prove to be an irresistible combination: the constant titillation that a man knew as much about the woman as she did herself! I'll bet he drives a scarlet Porsche or a white Jaguar, Fay thought derisively—a rakish, powerful sex symbol to complement his own big macho self-image! Oh, heavens, wouldn't it have been better to have stuck to her vague intention to occupy herself in London, rather than stay here, repeatedly trying to find answers to her own unwilling questions?

Still, she reassured herself, what did one day matter? So long as Craig kept his distance she could cope.

CHAPTER THREE

FAY was surprised to see that Craig's car was a vintage Railton in a restrained metallic grey that emphasised the long, tapering, riveted bonnet. It had an elegance that belonged to thoroughbreds of that era, and for a moment she stood admiring it, her own instinct for line and good design finding satisfaction in the sight. Then she looked up at Craig and smiled wryly; she might have guessed that he would come up with something utterly different, a rarity!

He caught her glance and nodded. 'An anachronism, I suppose,' he admitted, 'but my one extravagance. What's your extravagance?'

'I don't think I've got one,' she answered, settling into the low seat, breathing the scent of old, well-tended leather, and finding that the only comfortable position was with her legs outstretched.

'How bleak for you.' But he smiled, and after a moment Fay grinned as the car surged forward with a silent purr that proved the power of its eight cylinders.

Now that Brantye had been left behind, a weight seemed to be lifting from her shoulders. It was almost a holiday feeling, a sense of freedom, release. Around her the countryside was awakening to spring. Celandines shone on the grass verges, and in wooded clearings clumps of strap-like leaves promised later bluebells. The sun lit the walls of warm, Sussex brick, greened over with lichen as if the very fabric of the houses held a burgeoning fertility of its own. She stared out of the window, enjoying the peace, and for a while they drove in silence. Then Craig parked the car behind a small village, and they walked down the hill towards the main street.

Fay stopped, suddenly puzzled, before a house whose frontage had been extended. 'I'm sure this was a shop,' she began uncertainly. 'I used to buy sweets and a comic...'

Craig nodded, staring up at it. 'It was. But it's been gentrified. This is what's happening to villages all over the country as the commuter belt broadens.'

'And—wasn't that a school?' Fay exclaimed disbelievingly.

'And now it's a desirable residence,' Craig agreed. 'You just can't stop the tide.'

Arrested by a strange note in his voice, Fay glanced up at him. 'And—you care,' she said softly, after a moment. He looked down at her, an expression of self-mockery in his dark eyes. 'I mean—care about places... changing, dying out?' The revelation surprised her; somehow it seemed to bring them closer.

Then he shrugged philosophically. 'Some things, yes. Change for change's sake, especially when it sacrifices perfection, has got to be wrong. Still, it's progress, they tell us.'

As they turned away, he went on, 'Not to put too fine a point on it, I'm something of a conservationist. And naturally I'm sorry to see villages, which were once small worlds, become ornamental ghost towns between nine and five. You wouldn't believe it, but this place once had its own tailor, shoemaker, three butchers, a blacksmith...' Then he laughed, the skin around his eyes crinkling. 'But you get my drift, I'm sure, so I won't continue to ride my hobby-horse.'

Fay glanced about her, her eyes shadowed. 'It simply isn't the same place that I remember,' she said slowly. 'I'm not sure that I want to see any more.'

Craig half turned towards her, one eyebrow lifting quizzically. 'Don't tell me that you're feeling the pain of frustrated nostalgia!'

'No, not really,' Fay said practically. 'After all, it *is* years since I was here, and even then it was only in the school holidays. But somehow everything looks too—too tamed, too orderly, almost sterile.' She stared up the street. Apart from a girl with a child in a buggy outside a smart delicatessen which was new to Fay, she and Craig were the only people about. 'I suppose it just hasn't any relevance to me any more.'

'No, I see that. Your life is in Paris,' Craig reminded her, his eyes narrowing for a second.

'That's right.' Fay was surprised to hear the tart note in her voice. Surprised, too, to realise that for a while she seemed to have left Paris behind. The slightly wistful, partly pleasurable sensation of retracing old footsteps, even though the path *had* altered, coupled with the sheer Englishness of the landscape, and a baffling but growing sense of involvement with the man beside her, had driven her present and future way of life right out of her mind.

'Tell me about your job,' he said, as they got back into the car. 'Fashion, isn't it? Your sister said something that made it sound rather high-powered.'

'Yes, it's fashion. I'm a knitwear designer.'

'I can't imagine you knitting.' Craig smiled.

Fay laughed. 'Oh, I can knit. Not that I have to. Design is a matter of shapes, ideas, colours, imagination...'

'And you certainly have imagination,' he said, almost under his breath.

Fay flashed him a wary, defensive glance, but his face was bland. *He* should talk! His imagination had led him to some completely wrong ideas about her! However, better to dismiss that for the moment...

She glossed over her early years, then said thoughtfully, 'I was lucky, I guess. During college vacations I took jobs. I turned up at one firm with a portfolio of my designs under my arm, as a sort of testimony of my dedication, and I offered to do any job they could give me.' She smiled, her face softening reflectively, remembering the passion of her twenty-one-year-old self. Craig shot her a sideways glance and nodded, as if he, too, saw the same picture. 'At the end of that vacation they asked me to go back the following summer. They liked my designs and seemed to have taken a fancy to me. That's why I say I was lucky.'

'You must have earned your luck, though,' he remarked.

'I worked hard, yes. Anyway, when I went back the following year I shadowed one of the senior designers. I watched and listened, sat in on the edge of merchandising conferences—that kind of thing. They must have trusted me because a lot of it was highly confidential. It was a wonderful opportunity to see how things operated in the big world of business. At the end of that vacation they told me that there would be a place for me with the company when I finished my degree course.'

'A real success story,' Craig commented. 'You must have been pretty good.'

'We-ell...' Fay laughed. 'I was keen, enthusiastic.' There had also been a need to prove herself to Claudia. Her mind shied away from thoughts of her stepmother. 'I ate, drank, breathed knitwear. Then when they opened up in Paris I was sent there.'

'And obviously you enjoy it,' he said thoughtfully.

'Who wouldn't? Not that it doesn't have its headaches. Nor is it quite so glamorous as it probably sounds.'

He looked at her for a moment, a quick flick of darkness that took in every inch of her appearance, and Fay's pulse quickened maddeningly. She turned to stare out of the window. 'I *do* work hard, you know—occasionally right into the night if necessary, in a group project. And in the ideas stage I burn the midnight oil at home. And then there's the sheer, boring graft of working on the spec sheet—that's a flat drawing with measurements that goes to the manufacturer... But—oh, on the whole, it's exciting, creative, *challenging*. And there's plenty of travel. Sometimes I have to go to Hong Kong at a few days' notice, and there's the yarn fair in Florence...' She wished that the clamour inside would settle down, and she hurried on, a little breathlessly, 'And dyes—that's another thing: we don't use shade cards but create our own colours. It can be a long job, but when the dyers eventually come up with exactly the shade you want, then it's...'

He nodded. 'Exciting.'

She laughed, a little embarrassed. 'Yes. And I've gone on a bit, haven't I?'

'Enough to give me the general idea,' he said. 'And does your job provide you with *all* the excitement, all the colour you need? How about when you're *not* working?' Again, that sideways disturbing glance. His questions and his interest had seemed innocuous enough, even casual. But now she wondered if they covered some deeper, more subtle motive.

'Oh, I do the usual things, I suppose,' she hedged. 'There's no shortage of things to do in Paris.'

'Obviously.' He was silent for a moment, then he said suddenly, 'So there's not a chance of your holding on to Brantye?'

She stared at him in surprise. 'Not a chance,' she said decisively. 'The sooner it's sold, the better. I don't want to find myself having to foot various repair bills... Or perhaps that was Grandfather's intention,' she added with a half-laugh, 'to leave me a load of liabilities.'

She sensed rather than saw Craig's eyebrows knot into a quick scowl, and there was no mistaking the acerbity in his tone as he drawled, 'You appear to have an undeservedly low opinion of Julius.'

At a stroke that earlier animosity boiled up again, reminding Fay that this man had been inherently prejudiced against her from the start.

'I hardly knew him,' she answered shortly.

'No, you didn't,' Craig barked. 'Certainly not well enough to make such assumptions.'

'Oh, all right,' Fay said wearily, after a moment. 'I'm suitably chastened. Obviously you had a great affection for him.'

'Yes, I did. He was good to me.'

'And you owe him your loyalty, of course,' Fay murmured stiffly. 'In that case, I apologise. It was an unthinking remark which would have been better kept to myself.'

She shot him a covert glance, noting the hard, stubborn set of his jaw, the polish of light on his cheekbones, the firmly drawn black eyebrows. Clearly Craig Mackenzie wasn't a man to be crossed. And she had to admire his loyalty to her grandfather. Yes, perhaps he was right: her remark *had* been uncalled for. In an attempt to steer the conversation into calmer seas, she said lightly, 'You told me that you met Vicky at the funeral?'

His face relaxed a little as he nodded. 'Julius had mentioned her once or twice, of course, so when this—apparition appeared I identified her immediately.'

'Apparition?' Fay began to laugh. 'Oh, I see only too well!'

Craig's lingering severity dissolved in a smile. 'She had certainly dressed for the part. A long black cape over black boots, and the kind of hat you see in Thirties films. That was black, too. There were just two enormous blue eyes staring up from under the sweeping brim... She looked like a little girl dressing up. I found it rather endearing.'

Fay shook her head indulgently. 'As a potentially great dramatic actress Vicky never underestimates the value of impact. But it could have been worse, you know. In one of her psychedelic moods she might have considered a funeral the ideal scenario for introducing a note of eye-dazzling cheer. At least this time she observed the spirit of the occasion!'

'She sounds like fun,' Craig commented.

'She is. And as unpredictable as the weather.'

'Do I detect a note of envy?' he asked slyly.

'No, I don't think so. We're just very different, that's all.'

As they drove, Craig pointed out occasional landmarks. Then they turned into a narrow, twisting road, and in the distance Fay saw an old Sussex farmhouse, half timbered beneath its mellow stone tiles. As they approached up a well-tended gravel drive, the garden on each side fell away into a hollow of scree. Small statuettes were strategically placed among the stones and alpine plants, and at the bottom a shallow, thread-like stream whispered busily. Blue drifts of muscari caught Fay's eye, and the tiny 'hoop petticoat' narcissi, which her mother had loved, lay like spilt sunlight. 'How lovely,' she breathed.

'Yes, isn't it? There's an excellent restaurant, too. France doesn't quite have the monopoly, you know,' he smiled faintly.

'If I didn't think I knew you better,' Fay remarked, a teasing glint in her eyes, 'I might say that you were trying to impress me.'

He applied the handbrake without answering, but turned to give her a long, speculative glance that pulled a hot tide of blood into her face. She felt the prickling hush like something tangible within the car, and she got out quickly, flicking back her hair and concentrating on the scene around her with an exaggerated show of interest.

A few minutes later she was sipping an aperitif, relieved that they had got through the morning without Craig's having switched on too many of those disturbing, incomprehensible currents of sensation. But, in spite of her contrived calmness, she recognised all too well the force that lay just beneath the surface, beneath the apparently innocent conversation, ready to leap into life at his merest touch. And, apart from that one altercation about her grandfather, the time had passed very pleasantly. What a baffling man he was, Fay thought, eyeing him covertly as he studied the wine list. Intuitively, she sensed that there was so much more to him than his obvious attractiveness indicated. He would be difficult to know, and perhaps impossible to understand: a private person guarding his secret self under an exterior that sometimes brooded sombrely, but was sometimes lit by a quirky humour.

In Fay's fairly limited experience, many men might have capitalised on that tiny incident over the breakfast table, using it merely as an opening gambit, and moving right in with a swift follow-up. She was glad that Craig hadn't, she told herself decisively. And yet, still that perverse little needle of disappointment stabbed—that he hadn't felt the same explosive response.

It left her nonplussed, slightly off balance. She realised that she knew very little about him. He had encouraged her to talk of herself. That could have been a ploy to keep the conversational spotlight away from himself. But if so, why?

Again, in Fay's experience, men liked to talk about themselves. She had observed this often with Christophe. Christophe... He seemed to belong to another world. Right now he would be lunching in some smart Paris restaurant, immaculate in a dark suit with gleaming white shirt and subdued, expensive tie. She could almost see the glitter of his gold cufflinks above the strong, hairy wrists, and the large gold and onyx ring which had been passed down to him from that long-gone relation who had founded the family banking business.

Craig's voice cut across her thoughts, and she blinked. 'Sorry,' she murmured. 'I was miles away.'

'In Paris, no doubt.' His smile flickered briefly. 'I merely said that our table is ready.'

'In that case,' she answered brightly, 'let's eat.'

He stood up, and as if for the first time Fay experienced the tiny shock of his height. His pewter-coloured tweed suit was casual, yet it looked exactly right. She tried to imagine him unshaven, and in scruffy jeans, but even that couldn't detract from an impression of understated elegance. More likely, it would only emphasise the resolute jaw, and the sexuality of long legs and thighs that, while not over-muscled, swelled in a shallow arc of fluid strength. Watch it! she snapped silently. Do you actually *want* to find yourself out of your depth? And you certainly would be—with *this* man!

Deliberately she kept her talk general, laughing often, tossing small witticisms into the conversation until, when

Craig's eyebrows climbed quizzically, she caught herself up, murmuring brightly, 'I'm overdoing it again, I think. Blame it on the Chablis. I don't usually imbibe in the middle of the day.'

'Really?' He grinned. 'I thought it was an old French custom, a lingering lunch with wine?'

'Well, it might be for some. But for others like myself it's being replaced by a quick *croque-monsieur* from a fast food place.'

'What on earth is a *croque-monsieur*?' he asked with a laugh.

She pretended shock. She seemed to be doing rather a lot of pretending, she realised. 'Your education's sadly lacking,' she mocked. 'It's a toasted cheese and ham sandwich.'

She glanced around at the gleaming napery, the bright silver and sparkling glass, at the smattering of business-men, and the few elderly couples—the wives re-strainedly jewelled. Her eyes lingered on a table where eight younger, well-dressed women were obviously en-joying some kind of celebration. 'Do you come here often?' she asked, then laughed. 'Sorry, I didn't mean that to sound quite as gauche as it did; it was just a natural progression from the *croque-monsieur*. I mean, this could hardly be a greater contrast to my usual lunch hour.'

'No, I rarely eat here,' he answered. 'Tell me, is there such a thing as a *croque-madame*?'

'Oh, yes,' Fay answered blithely. 'But that has an egg in it as well.' Suddenly embarrassed, she felt herself blushing hotly. The remark seemed almost sexually in-timate, as if it embodied the whole wonderful physical make-up of woman, and man's involvement.

But Craig merely gave an amused laugh. 'Shall we take coffee in the palm house?' He stood up and came to draw out her chair before the waiter could reach them. For a moment their fingers touched as he passed her handbag up. Fay found herself lost for words in the renewed turbulence. Be your age! she told herself crossly, twisting away. His hand fell, but not before she had seen his enigmatic smile. She stared at him stonily, but his expression didn't change.

As they took their seats on white cane chairs amid luxurious greenery, he said, 'I don't want to harp on things, but it really *is* definite that you'll be getting rid of Brantye?'

She looked at him sharply, trying to pin down feelings which had a thistledown craziness and were leading her in a completely wrong direction. 'Why, yes. I thought I'd made that absolutely clear. I'm surprised that you should ask.' Here, at least, was a safe topic of conversation, she thought with a sense of relief.

He shrugged. 'I was just wondering how it would be if we were—neighbours. You in the big house, me at The Lodge . . .'

'Tugging your forelock each time I drove through the gates? I can't imagine it, somehow.' She laughed, paused, then went on flatly, 'It's quite out of the question for me to do anything else but sell the place. My work—and my home,' she added, with slight emphasis, 'and my life, come to that, isn't here.'

'But all that could be changed.'

She put down her cup and stared at him. 'Now why on earth would I want to alter a situation which I find entirely satisfactory?' Surely he couldn't be suggesting that she gave up everything merely to be his *neighbour*? Even *he* couldn't be *that* arrogant!

'Oh, it occurred to me that you might be considering starting up on your own, working under your own label. People do, you know. And Brantye would make a pretty impressive base.' He stood up abruptly. 'Or don't your ambitions extend that far?'

Still staring, Fay got up. 'It's out of the question,' she said vehemently. 'Completely——'

'Why?' he said, very softly. 'Could it be that as an employ*ee*—rather than an employ*er*—you feel safe? Secure?'

Damn, she thought, why did he have to probe so? She swallowed and said haughtily, 'I doubt if there's such a thing as absolute security in the field of fashion design—or in anything else, come to that.'

'But if there were, then that's what you would lean towards? Tell me, Fay, does that unadventurous spirit affect other areas of your life, too?'

Words sprang into her mouth, angry, tumbling, incoherent, and she bit her lip firmly. At her silence he merely smiled triumphantly. She tried to look impassive. She would *not* allow him the satisfaction of goading her. What right had he to scratch the surface in this way? Holding up her sensible, practical attitudes as if they were shabby garments?

'Where are we going now?' she asked stiffly, after a while.

'To blow away the effects of that meal, clear your head of the wine fumes,' he said lightly.

'I'm not *that* fogged,' she said, adding pointedly, 'I *do* know what I'm doing, you know.'

'Of course you do,' he soothed. 'I can't imagine any situation where you didn't know *exactly* what you were doing.'

'Well, you don't have to make it sound so contemptible,' she muttered.

He dropped a light hand on her knee for a fraction of a second. 'Come on, stop being so disgruntled. Let's enjoy what's left of the day, shall we? Just think, in another couple of days you'll be back, snug in your little cocoon again,' he mocked.

'All right!' she said hotly. 'I *will* enjoy the rest of the day. And I *will* be back, snug in my own cocoon, as you disparagingly phrase it, in a couple of days. And you know why? Because that's how I like it, how I *want* it. I *chose* it! And now can we change the subject? How about *your* little cocoon?'

He laughed indulgently. 'What do you want to know about me? Fire away.'

'We-ell, when you put it like that—I don't know. We might as well start with your work. How did you get into it?'

For a time he spoke of his training, of Julius's wise counsel, of his long apprenticeship with a fine arts dealer. In a sense, Fay realised, interested despite herself, his initiation had been similar to hers. But she hadn't had a mentor like Julius; she had had to fight every inch of the way against Claudia's gently expressed objections, soliciting her father's help, and thereby driving a greater wedge into family relationships.

They were high up on the Downs now, with the countryside below spreading towards the Channel in a haze of green and brown. 'Let's walk for a while,' Craig said, getting out of the car.

Up here the wind was strong, snatching their breath so that talk was difficult. Fay found it exhilarating, feeling her hair lift and stream out behind her. Leaning into the wind, they rounded a small bluff where, in the shelter, the air was suddenly calm. Still braced against the wind's force, Fay was almost thrown off balance. 'Steady,' Craig said, his arm suddenly cradling her shoulders. She straightened. Then it happened. She was close to him, rough tweed grazing her cheek. In the same moment she looked up blindly, and his mouth came down on hers with a hard deliberation that annihilated her conventional, half-hearted protests.

His lips were warm, with a deep sweetness that seemed to search out her core, lifting her heart and setting it beating to a mad, intoxicating rhythm. His arms closed around her more tightly, pressing her body against his own in a silent statement of possession. When his mouth finally left hers, her whole body throbbed, and had it not been for his arms around her she might have fallen. Never had she experienced a sensation so completely devastating. For a moment she hid her face against his shoulder, not daring to look at him, unable to believe the intensity of her response.

Instinctively she had guessed that it would be like this; some primitive wisdom had warned her that this man was unique. Somehow she had recognised in her soul that his body lodged a force that would assail and shock, leaving her trembling and troubled and unsure, exactly as she was now. But she had never dreamed that there could be so much magic in a mere kiss.

His hand moved up, turning her face towards him again, but she resisted, trying to marshal all her forces against him, pushing her forehead into his shoulder for support. Then, after a moment, he held her away from him. Her eyes were still downcast; she was still trying to hide his effect upon her.

'Hmm,' he said softly, 'I had a feeling that somewhere under all that polish there was a warm, human woman trying to get out.'

She stepped back swiftly, half stumbling to get out of his reach, furious with herself and with him. 'Well, good for you!' she whispered brokenly. 'You simply can't resist plumbing the—the depths to see what you might find, can you? Well, let me tell you something: you're beginning to sound like some badly scripted soap opera.

You seem to think you have a magic key, an Open Sesame to what goes on under my skin!'

'You're not doing too badly yourself in the corny script stakes,' he answered, infuriatingly cool. Then his voice roughened cruelly. 'Tell me, Fay, is there something *wrong* with warm, human women? Is it a weakness in your book to have ordinary human emotions?'

'Of course not,' she snapped. 'I just happen to prefer to keep them to myself, and——'

'Until a moment like that happens,' he murmured, 'which, by definition, has to be shared. And then you can't help yourself.'

Angry beyond all speech, she glared at him. But he was right, damn it! And he was the very last type of person to whom she should reveal her true, inner self. Already he seemed to know too much about her.

'You had it all set up, didn't you?' she breathed at last. 'You disliked me from the moment I walked into Brantye. You saw me as greedy, avaricious. You thought I had come to gloat over my inheritance, to figure out how much it was worth. And you resented it with all your heart because my grandfather and I were virtual strangers. You've lost no opportunity to deride me and the way I live, the way I haven't let memories and nostalgia bog me down. So you engineered a pleasant morning drive, a very nice lunch and this—this *walk*,' she ended scornfully. 'You make me want to——' She stopped suddenly at the sight of his face.

His features held all the coldness of steel. His brows were drawn so thunderously that two small indentations appeared above them on his forehead. When he spoke his words rasped from barely parted lips. 'Did I?' he said, his voice dangerously quiet. 'I went to all that trouble just so that I could kiss you? Is that what you're saying? Heavens above, but you certainly flatter yourself!'

'No,' Fay flung back. 'I *don't* flatter myself. You were merely settling an old score.'

'Oh, lord,' he breathed disgustedly, 'what a strange, twisted mind you have.' He reached out, his fingers digging into her shoulders, dragging her savagely around to face him. 'I kissed you because I wanted to.' One imperious finger jerked her chin up, and she found her baffled eyes imprisoned by his penetrating gaze. 'Is that so hard to understand?'

'It's completely *impossible* to understand exactly what gives you the right! Some divine providence, I suppose.' She heard her own words with a sense of disbelief. Why, for heaven's sake, was she making such heavy weather of it? It was nothing. It *had* to mean nothing... And talking about it only made it important and left her feeling even more confused—about him, about herself. About every damn thing!

'We'd better go,' she said in a dead voice. 'Suddenly London is the one place I long to be.'

'Next to Paris, of course,' he taunted.

They walked in a thick silence, and once in the car Fay leaned back in the seat. Anger still vibrated through her. She stared out of the window, her eyes dry and hard. She had made too much of a production of the whole thing. Handled it quite wrongly. It would have been better to laugh and walk away. Laugh? How could she, when she still seemed to feel the warmth of his lips, the fire in her body which she tried desperately to repudiate?

'Look,' he said blandly after a while, 'so we got off to a bad start. Hadn't we better forget it?' He drew the car over on to a grass verge and turned to face her. Fay shrank away, and his face hardened again.

'I intend to forget—everything,' she answered.

'Strange woman,' he mused impassively. 'You wanted that kiss, so stop pretending. I felt it on your lips.'

'You really do have the monopoly of sheer male vanity,' she said crushingly. Then, as he opened his mouth to speak, she went on, 'And there's nothing to discuss. All right, so you kissed me. There's nothing so special about that—only the motives behind it. I *have* been kissed before, you know, but for the *right* reasons. Not by someone who nurses a bitterness against me simply because of an inheritance. And that says it all. Now, do you think we might get back *quickly*? I'm in a hurry.'

Without speaking he swung the car on to the road again. The way ahead stretched clear and straight, and the car surged forward on a mounting tide of quiet power. Fay's knuckles whitened as she gripped the edges of her seat. Craig gave a hard, mirthless laugh. 'Anything to oblige a lady,' he murmured. 'You asked for speed, and now you've got it. There's an old proverb about being careful with your wishes in case they're granted.'

'You have all the answers,' Fay said scathingly.

'I do my best,' he agreed, his voice smooth as cream. But after a moment his foot eased off the accelerator and Fay was able to relax a little.

'There are moments when I find you very easy to—to—hate,' she said in a strangled voice as they neared Brantye.

'Really?' he drawled interestedly. 'But why the aggression? What's bugging you, Fay?' His half-smile goaded and infuriated her.

'Don't tell me that your infallible power of discernment has deserted you at last,' she said spikily. 'The fact that we don't exactly hit it off doesn't necessarily mean that I have some peculiar quirk, some hang-up.

You don't have to dig so deep into my psyche to find the answer. It's simple, really—you meet people, and some you like, and some you don't. It happens all the time. Or hadn't you noticed?' She was aware that she sounded mean and waspish, but if it helped to keep him at arm's length then so be it.

'Oh, well,' he said resignedly, 'at least I did attempt to penetrate that thorny hedge you've built around yourself.'

'It was a waste of time,' she snapped.

He braked suddenly at the big iron gates. 'Was it?' he gritted. 'I wonder.' Then he cupped her jaw, savagely jerking her head round to face him. 'I don't easily admit defeat...' Then his head came down swiftly, blotting out the blue spring sky as he swept her to him with resolute strength.

'No——!' She tried to wrench her face away.

'Oh, *yes*,' he hissed against her lips. 'Yes and yes and *yes*!'

An involuntary stifled moan broke from her. She felt battered, bruised and limp. There was no fight left in her now. He was too much. A half-sob of despair parted her lips.

The violence had gone out of him now, leaving only the intoxication of a demanding mouth silently persuading her that only *this* mattered. His thumbs caressed the sweep of her throat, softly touching the lobes of her ears. 'Fay...' he said thickly. 'For heaven's sake... When something strange and beautiful happens, grab it, celebrate it.'

She barely heard his words. All her senses were fused into the single one of touch, and when his tongue flicked into the dark warmth of her mouth she gave a convulsive shudder, her arms moving, her fingers groping blindly in his strong, thick hair. She felt his gasp, the sudden spasm of his body as his hands moved down over her neck to peel away the soft wool cowl. In exactly the same way, she thought deliriously, as he was peeling away the conventional, hard-held layers of herself. His lips broke away to trace the line of her neck, finally resting in the hollow of her throat. She could smell his hair, an outdoor scent faintly underlain by an elusive herby fragrance. As he cupped her breasts, the sweet, desperate longing inside her surged even more strongly.

She felt his palms, warm through the green wool, as if they melted her, and she drew his head up so that he might find her lips again, this time ready, wanting... Sensations which had for so long been consciously buried now surfaced dizzyingly.

At last he drew away from her. She looked up into his eyes. So dark! Unreadable in their intensity. 'Just think,' he said, softly taunting, 'what marvellous neighbours we *might* have been. Oh, all right; I know what you said.' As he started the motor, he went on, 'I expect to be in Paris in a couple of weeks. We might meet, perhaps?'

Fay nodded mutely. She seemed to have been taken over.

'Good.' His hand came down to give her knee a powerful squeeze. She didn't wince. She knew now that she wanted him—all of him: his strength, his authority, his—mystery. For better or for worse, in hostility or in peace.

She sighed and sat back. She still throbbed with the sensations he had aroused in her. In just twenty-four hours he had turned her world upside-down, inside out. She wasn't the same person who had arrived at Brantye the previous day.

Gently he let in the clutch as they turned into the drive.

Beside the car which Fay had hired stood another, identical to it. She looked at Craig, bewildered. 'Am I...?

I'm not seeing double, am I? Are you expecting——?' Then she stopped, her words cut off sharply as his face changed. From the impassive mask she read nothing, only noticed a tightening of the sensuous, pleasure-giving mouth, a secrecy in the dark, alert eyes.

At that moment a woman stepped back from the porch, her hand raised to greet them. With a disbelief that stunned her, Fay recognised her stepmother, Claudia.

CHAPTER FOUR

ELEGANT as always, Claudia came slowly down the steps towards them. As she moved, the loose panels of her shaded cream silk dress floated around her exquisite legs like petals. The matching corded-silk jacket accentuated her pale golden tan and biscuit-coloured hair, beautifully cut in a smooth Dutch bob. She looked youthful and vibrant and incredibly poised, Fay thought through her shock of disbelief.

'Why, *Fay*!' Claudia exclaimed softly, offering her cheek for a kiss. 'I didn't expect to find *you* here.'

'Oh? Weren't you looking . . . wanting to see me?' Fay said feebly, trying to recover her composure. She caught a breath of Je Reviens—a perfume she would always associate with Claudia.

'No, my dear. At least—not *today*.'

As if hypnotised Fay's eyes followed Claudia's movements round to the driver's side of the car where, raising high-arched feet out of delicate court shoes, Claudia reached up to kiss Craig's cheek. 'I've been wondering where on earth you were, Craig,' she said, lightly reproving. 'I tried The Lodge but it was locked . . . I got away from the wedding earlier than I expected, so I came straight over. It was a beautiful reception, but quite exhausting . . .' She laughed. 'Now don't tell me that you've forgotten our dinner date!'

'How could I?' Craig said urbanely. 'I simply took Fay to look around her old haunts, and——'

'And I've just called in to collect my case.' Fay heard the brusqueness in her tone. The sense of doom provoked by Claudia's sudden appearance completely eclipsed the awakening joy offered so briefly in the past few minutes. 'My car's here, you see...' she finished lamely.

Claudia looked like a sunbeam in the dark house, Fay thought dully, as they stood uncertainly in the hall. She couldn't bring herself to look at Craig; the fact that he and Claudia were on fairly familiar terms had struck her like a body-blow, and she was still reeling.

'Oh, must you go?' Claudia said, breaking an awkward silence. 'It's so long since we had a chat, and, although I'm as surprised to see you here today as, apparently, you are to see me, I admit that I *have* been wanting to have a word.'

'Then why not kill two birds with one stone?' Craig suggested pleasantly. 'Stay a while, Fay. You two can do your talking while I rustle up a pot of tea. Come over to The Lodge when you're ready.'

'That's a wonderful idea,' Claudia approved. 'All that champagne has made me thirsty, and——'

'Sorry, but I simply must be on my way,' Fay said.

Claudia gave a regretful sigh. 'She's an elusive creature. Do you know, Craig, despite the fact that we both live in France I don't see much of her. But then,' she laughed, with a little admonitory tap on Fay's wrist, 'you're so very busy with your exciting career, aren't you?'

Fay said nothing, feeling her smile set like a death mask on her face.

'Are you going straight back to Paris?' Claudia pursued. 'If so, what a pity it is that we can't travel together. However, I *do* have one or two matters to see to while I'm over here, and old friends——' she flashed Craig a warmly inclusive glance '—to look up.'

Suddenly Fay couldn't bear to be in the same room as them both. There seemed something horribly false about the whole situation. 'I'm spending a day or so with Vicky before I go back home,' she said abruptly, and turned to run up the stairs.

She heard Craig's footsteps behind her just before he overtook her on the gallery. 'I'll get your case,' he said, loud enough for Claudia to hear. Then, swiftly, 'I believe I know what you're thinking.'

'Even *you* can't be that intuitive,' Fay whispered with a false, bright smile. 'And I *am* capable of carrying my own case, thank you.'

Her heart was thumping painfully, but that seemed to be the only sign of life in her body. Everything else was numb; that amazing elation she had known in Craig's arms only minutes ago was snuffed out as irrevocably as if it had never been.

He stared at her for a moment, then his eyes narrowed. 'I see...' he said tautly. 'Suddenly you simply can't wait to get away. Well, don't let me detain you. As you're in such a tearing hurry the least I can do is bring your car round to the door. And—Fay, thanks for the interlude.'

Fay saw the rigid line of his mouth, the scornful glint in his eyes. She was aware, too, of Claudia below, her face lifted towards them in a gentle blur of amusement. 'Oh, by the way,' Craig resumed, with a soft, poisonous sting in his voice, 'don't forget to take your roses.'

In the bedroom Fay pressed icy knuckles against her hot face. Damn him. That parting shot had been delivered like an insult.

Claudia's words rang on and on in her head: '...old friends to look up...' Her meaning had been clear. So, Fay thought slowly, small wonder that Craig had brought the conversation round to the subject of Claudia the previous evening. Skilfully he had drawn out Fay's confidences. He had listened in silence, and in some way which she couldn't define had given the impression that he didn't know Claudia, that he had only seen her on that one occasion when Fay's father and Julius had quarrelled. And, like a fool, Fay hadn't bothered to conceal her antipathy towards Claudia.

She gave a short laugh of self-contempt, then went over to the dressing-table and automatically combed her hair and renewed her lipstick. Her composure was returning, bred out of that firm self-control behind which she had preserved herself over the years, particularly where Claudia was concerned.

She went down by the back stairs, and when she came out of the kitchen carrying her flowers Claudia was alone, stretched out on a sofa, her shoes kicked off, massaging her toes. 'Bliss to get my feet off the ground,' she murmured. 'And what heavenly roses! Something tells me that you didn't buy them for yourself.'

Fay was able to summon up a smile. 'Then that something tells you the truth.'

Claudia laughed. 'You were always a mysterious creature,' she said tolerantly.

'Oh, no mystery,' Fay answered. 'And they're not from Craig, if that's what you're wondering.'

'Ah. A Paris boyfriend, perhaps. I assume there is one?'

'Your car's outside,' Craig put in baldly from the doorway.

'Oh, very much so, Claudia. You must meet him some time,' Fay added politely. Then she turned to Craig. 'Thank you,' she said brightly. 'I don't remember Brantye offering such good service in the old days. But then, so much has changed, hasn't it? And thanks for the Memory Lane trip, even if it *was* a disappointment. Well... Goodbye, Claudia.'

'Short and sweet, but I'll be in touch soon.' Claudia got up, sliding her feet into the tiny court shoes. 'I'll come out and wave you on your way.'

Fay managed to retain her smile, relieved not to be alone with Craig. When she reached the car he was holding open the door. 'Be careful how you drive,' he said politely, his arm brushing hers.

'Have no fear!' Fay exclaimed. 'If the Paris *périphérique* holds no terrors for me, then I'm quite sure I can cope with the Sussex lanes. I'm a survivor. Or hadn't you noticed?' she added with a laugh.

'Oh, no, you mustn't worry about Fay,' Claudia confirmed sunnily, linking her arm through Craig's. 'She's a wonderful driver and just about the most independent girl I've ever known.' She leaned into the car, investing it with her perfume, to drop a light kiss on Fay's cheek. 'I haven't told you how pleased I am for you—about your inheritance,' she said. 'I'm sure we have lots to talk about, but we'll get together soon.'

Fay nodded woodenly and released the handbrake. For a while she drove automatically, until she was surprised to feel tears on her cheeks. She pulled over into the gateway of a field. She was being utterly, incredibly juvenile! Tears for her were a rare indulgence and warranted a far worthier cause than Craig Mackenzie! Yet she couldn't dispel the numbing depression that had closed in on her.

Just what *was* the connection between him and Claudia? Nothing in his conversation over dinner the previous evening had suggested that he and Claudia were old friends, so why had he deliberately misled Fay?

Of course, she thought wearily, if he *was* seriously interested in Claudia, that would explain why he had brought up her name: obviously he had wanted to hear about her. Fay sniffed, blotting her cheeks. After all,

Claudia was extremely attractive and very, very feminine—probably just the kind of woman to appeal to a man like Craig. And the age difference was negligible; Claudia was his senior by only a couple of years.

Fay groped in her handbag for her cologne stick and stroked it refreshingly over her forehead. She would wipe out the last two days. Forget them completely. Whatever the situation was between Craig and Claudia, it had nothing to do with *her*. And, all things considered, perhaps it was providential that Claudia had come upon the scene just when she did, illustrating only too clearly that Craig had merely been amusing himself with Fay. Maybe, after Claudia's melting femininity, Fay's cool, self-contained manner had been a challenge which his macho self-image couldn't resist. So surely it was better to know all this now rather than later, by which time her emotions might have led her into a deeper commitment. Her resistance to him was too weak. But then, he was that kind of man. Too positive an impact, she decided miserably.

'An interlude.' That was how he had dismissed those vibrant, thrilling moments. And that was how she, too, would dismiss them.

When Fay let herself into Vicky's flat she saw that her sister's departure had been too hurried to impose any kind of order on the place. It was a relief to have something to tackle physically, and as Fay tidied the room and put things to rights in the kitchen her wild experience with Craig began to recede like a bizarre, improbable dream.

With the flat at last presentable, Fay went out to a Greek delicatessen which appeared to stay open twenty-four hours a day, bought bread and pâté and freshly ground coffee and returned to curl up in an armchair with a tray beside her, trying to concentrate on a television play.

Vicky banged into the flat the following day just before lunch. 'We're celebrating,' she said, without ceremony, hugging Fay and bouncing up and down. 'I'm opening in *Hobson's Choice* in two weeks. So come on, I'm taking you out to Bruno's. I can afford it, you know, thanks to Grandfather.' She blew a kiss into the air and laughed. 'What super roses! Did you buy them for *me*?'

Fay smiled. Vicky always had a tonic effect upon her. 'Hardly. Christophe bought them for *me*, but I've no intention of carrying them back to Paris, so they're all yours.'

'Christophe?' Vicky's mobile features flashed into a grimace. 'You're still seeing him, then?'

'I am,' Fay said emphatically. 'And why not?'

'Well, he's——' Vicky twirled round in an excess of energy, then fell on to the sagging sofa '—stuffy. I mean, you don't expect a Frenchman to be...stuffy.' She jumped up. 'I'll go and change. I feel a bit crumpled.' As she passed the small table near the window, she kissed the tip of her forefinger and touched the framed photograph of their mother. Then, noticing Fay's face, she said sheepishly, 'Silly, isn't it, but—I feel that she helps me. I muffed my lines, and I knew I hadn't a chance. Sudden death... Then this fierce-looking guy smiled and said, "I think you'll do, Miss Armitage."'

Fay stared after her thoughtfully. That little gesture had been revealingly poignant. Vicky had been only seven when their mother died, and for a time had become very withdrawn. She'd had frightening nightmares, Fay recalled—nights when she, only three years older, had crept into her sister's bed to try and offer comfort out of her own grief.

She picked up the photograph and looked into the eyes so like her own. How different things might have been!

She blinked as Vicky called gaily, 'I'll be able to keep this flat on—for a while, anyway, until I know what's what, thanks to Grandfather's legacy.'

Later, as Bruno put their lasagne before them, Vicky said, 'I've been doing all the talking. Your turn now. What did you think of Brantye? Gloomy old place, isn't it? Of course, I don't have so many happy memories of it as you do, but I went over to take a look at it after Grandfather's funeral.'

'I shall sell it,' Fay said decisively. 'The land, at least, must bc valuablc.'

'Well, get it on the market soon, before the chimneys fall down,' Vicky grinned with a sudden streak of practicality. 'There just might be someone, somewhere, who would like to turn it into a health farm or a conference centre. By the way,' she added casually, scooping up the last of the creamy sauce with an expression of ecstasy, 'did you meet Craig Mackenzie? Grandfather's old protégé. He lives at The Lodge, apparently.'

'Yes, I met him.'

Something in Fay's voice prompted Vicky to look up quickly.

'And obviously you weren't very impressed.'

'Should I have been?' Fay stalled, taking a sip of wine.

'We-ell, *I* thought he was quite something—if you're into that age group, of course,' Vicky added with a mischievous grin. 'Actually he drove me back to my flat after the funeral—rather nice of him, wasn't it? I found him very easy to talk to.'

'So, apparently, does Claudia,' Fay remarked smoothly. 'When I left yesterday afternoon Claudia had just arrived. Obviously they know each other very well.'

Vicky gave a low whistle. 'Really? I wouldn't have said that Claudia was his style at all.' She frowned thoughtfully. 'Small world, though. I mean, there's this guy, Craig, sort of related to us in an involved kind of way through Grandfather. And there's our stepmother, and, even though family ties are frail, to put it mildly, these two know each other. Still,' she shrugged, 'it happens, I suppose. Perhaps Claudia met him among the fleshpots of the Riviera. After all, he's not the kind of fella one could overlook. And you have to hand it to Claudia—she's no one's idea of the pathetic little widow, even if that is the line she seems to be taking.'

'Is she?' Fay's eyebrows rose in surprise. 'That's not the way she was acting when I left her at Brantye.' She stirred her coffee unseeingly. 'She looked very glamorous and entirely self-assured.'

'She's short of money,' Vicky said succinctly. 'And she can put on quite a convincing show of pathos... You know the patter—lonely widow, shrinking capital, not to mention that disastrous boutique business she went into... I needn't go on.'

'And that's why she came to see *you*,' Fay said quietly.

'I rather think so. After all, she's never shown much interest in me before, but now that I'm solvent...'

Fay nodded. 'I see. And she would know about your inheritance probably through Craig. Yes, I think I do see.'

'Finished? Then let's go. I feel that I deserve a shopping spree, and I've found a marvellous dress agency with some real period pieces. You can give me your Paris-flavoured advice. And who knows, you may get some inspiration for your next collection? And no,' Vicky added firmly as Fay opened her handbag, 'this is *my* treat. You hold on to your money, because I can't help feeling that money is behind Claudia's wish to see *you*. I'm surprised she didn't tackle you yesterday.'

'I guess she had other things on her mind,' Fay answered lightly.

Vicky laughed. 'Craig, you mean? Well, say what you like about Claudia, she's always had good taste.'

'I think,' Vicky said, two hours later as they left the dress shop, each clutching a large bag, 'I shall give a party tonight to celebrate. Nothing fancy, just wine and bits to eat. You're good at doing those. A nice little impromptu affair. I'll ring around when I get back.'

Fay looked at her and began to laugh. 'Vicky, you do me a world of good,' she said.

Vicky looked pleased. 'How so? You—I mean, you always seem so...so in charge—as if you don't need anything from *anyone*. Mind,' she added thoughtfully, 'I did think you had a touch of the Brantye blues earlier. Never mind. Sell it, then you can set up on your own.'

'How odd!' Fay exclaimed before she could stop herself. 'Craig Mackenzie said almost the same thing, except that he suggested I work from Brantye.'

'Perhaps he has designs on you.' Vicky gave a peal of laughter. 'Pardon the pun. But you would be neighbours then. An intriguing prospect. Isn't it worth thinking about?'

Vicky seemed to be echoing Craig's words, Fay thought dully, but she forced a laugh. 'Absolutely not. I'm very happy in Paris. Now, don't you think we ought to call in at that delicatessen and see about some food for this party of yours?'

By midnight the walls of Fay's flat seemed to reverberate with noise. 'Aren't you worried about the neighbours complaining?' Fay asked as she opened more wine in the cluttered kitchen.

'Relax. They're the ones who are making the din. I took the precaution of inviting them. You know, Fay, you look stunning. I'm so glad you let me persuade you into buying that dress.'

Fay laughed. Somehow, through Vicky, she had managed to salvage something happy and heart-warming from the depressing chore of coming to England to see Mr Seymour, the gloom of Brantye, and her utterly worthless and humiliating encounter with Craig Mackenzie. All of which had left her feeling rather cheap. Not to mention the meeting with Claudia which, as always, was disturbing. But tonight all those things were behind her, and tomorrow she would be back in Paris.

Still laughing, she lifted her arms and the gauzy blue sleeves fell away like fragile wings. She pirouetted so that the flounced skirt spun, its silver threads catching the light like rippling water.

A smatter of applause came from the doorway, and Fay froze suddenly, a great boulder in her chest cutting off her breath.

Craig Mackenzie stood there watching her, a faint smile on his lips, his eyes like warm, thrilling secrets.

'Bravo!' he murmured. 'Beautifully executed.' Then he looked from Fay to Vicky. 'I *did* knock,' he said suavely, 'but the door was open anyway.'

'Come along in,' Vicky said delightedly. 'How nice to see you! Join the party. I believe that you and Fay have already met. Fay,' she said, turning and ignoring Fay's flaming face, 'get our guest a drink, will you, while I hunt out that Roberta Flack tape?'

When she had gone, the silence seemed to throb as loudly as the rock music.

'Red or white?' Fay said politely, at last.

'Red, please. Here, let me do it. You don't have to stand on ceremony, you know. After all, it isn't as if we had just met. Is it?' he pressed softly.

Fay stood back, ignoring the question. After a moment she said coolly, 'You're having a hectic couple of days, it seems. Lunch with me, dinner with Claudia, and now Fay's party. What a wild social round you do have.'

'Oh, I get about a bit,' he remarked modestly.

Fay gave a brittle laugh. 'I'm quite sure you do.'

He regarded her over the rim of his glass, then took a small, wry sip. 'But I don't have to tell you that I didn't come here for the party.'

'I realise that,' Fay retorted. 'You couldn't have known there *was* a party. So just why *did* you come?' She concentrated on maintaining a glacial calm, but in spite of her efforts an erratic little pulse beat maddeningly in her throat, doing strange things to her breathing. The kitchen light was cruelly revealing, and so was the neckline of her dress. No doubt Craig was well aware of her nervousness. 'Well?' she snapped, when he didn't answer.

'You left a comb and a lipstick in your room at Brantye,' he murmured silkily.

'And you've brought them all this way?' Fay gave a breathy, derisive laugh. 'How kind! But rather unnecessary. I do have other lipsticks and other combs. However, thank you.' She held out her hand.

'Also,' he went on imperturbably, 'I found a little pink lustre dish in one of the cupboards. Vicky happened to mention that she collects pink lustre.' He took a flat parcel from one of his pockets.

'Well, if you want to give it to her you know where she is.' Fay turned away to collect a few corks and throw them in the waste bin.

'However, there was another reason,' he said, placing the dish at the back of the worktop. 'I wanted to see you.'

'So now you do,' Fay told him flippantly. 'And you'll also see that I'm rather busy.' She turned away again, wishing that she could feel as detached and disinterested as her words suggested. Craig was wearing a suit of fine, dark cloth in a muted bird's-eye weave, a pristine white shirt and grey silk tie. The conventional clothes served only to emphasise the almost gypsyish darkness of his eyes and hair, the hard power of his body. Fay tried to thrust away the memory of his arms around her, the touch and smell of him, and, forcing a note of boredom into her voice, she said, 'I doubt very much if this is your scene, so if you want to go, feel free.'

'You know something?' he said conversationally, putting down his glass and folding his arms across his chest as he lounged against the kitchen unit. 'A few hours ago I would have said that it wasn't quite *your* scene either. Only now,' he went on softly, lowering his eyelids in a look so sensual that she felt it shiver over her skin, 'seeing you, watching you move in that dress . . . I'm not so certain.' His voice bit suddenly. 'Doesn't that prove that we shouldn't make sweeping judgements?'

'Oh, well,' she dismissed, 'we're all more than one person.'

'What an astute remark!' he mocked, his mouth twisting. 'There are certain times, Fay, when I——'

He broke off as Vicky came into the kitchen. 'Oh, come on, you two,' she said gaily. 'This is a party, and I want to get them dancing instead of just standing around.'

'A good idea,' Craig answered smoothly. 'Fay?' He raised questioning eyebrows, but his arm across her shoulders was a compulsion written in fire as he propelled her through into the other room, and she found herself with no option but to turn and go into his arms.

She tried to hold herself stiffly away from him, cursing Vicky's manipulation, and hoping that her aversion would communicate itself to Craig. But his face was bland, and when he laid his cheek against her hair she could only try to smother a frightening sense of panic, wishing that the music would stop, or that someone would change the tape back to a rock number. But the soft, plaintive notes flowed out, insidiously weakening her resolve so that she was painfully conscious of her clamouring senses.

The room was crowded, but when they were able to move a little Craig's thigh brushed her own. The feel of his hands on skin bared by the low-cut back of her dress seemed to scorch her, and when his fingers began to stroke with feathering movements she felt as if she were being attacked by some impossibly tender yet lethal weapon. She missed her step and pulled away hurriedly. 'Sorry, but I don't much care for dancing,' she lied, 'so——'

Instantly his hands dropped. 'So we'll sit this one out? Certainly. We'll talk instead.'

'Now look,' she said, a note of wildness slashing her voice, 'I'm supposed to be in charge of the catering. And... There are—things to... More drinks. I must open some more——'

'But of course,' he said maddeningly. 'I'll help you. I have a strong wrist. Come along, Fay. What are you afraid of?'

She glared at him. Dancing with him was dangerous enough, but being alone and talking to him was just as bad. Why couldn't he leave her alone? He had had his fun, hadn't he? 'Look,' she said tightly, 'you've delivered the—the goods, and I'm grateful. And I'm sure Vicky will be delighted with the dish.' Desperately she tried to catch Vicky's eye and beckon her over, but Vicky was engrossed in conversation with a small group. Defeated, Fay turned back to face him. 'But you have a long drive back,' she resumed, 'so don't let me detain you.'

'Why not?' Again, his gaze cruised slowly over her. 'There's nothing I'd like better than for you to—detain me. I had thought that yesterday you almost accepted that.' As if to endorse his words he reached for her hand, cradling it in both of his, stroking each finger slowly in a sensual, lulling rhythm.

Fay drew a ragged breath and snatched her hand away. 'Spare me any more of that corny dialogue, will you?' she flared. 'Can't you see that you're not wanted here?'

'No?' he breathed. 'As I said earlier, your face is more honest than your words. I also told you that I don't easily accept defeat. Unlike you.'

'What's that supposed to mean?' she scoffed. 'I'm not defeated. How can I be, when there is no contest?'

'No,' he affirmed, 'there's no contest, but in spite of your words you seem to think there is.'

'Oh, just go away,' she snapped, closing her eyes. 'I was enjoying myself until you came.' Tears of frustration stung her eyelids and she turned quickly away. But his hands came down hard on her shoulders, swinging her around to face him.

'What are you afraid of?' he said softly. His face was so close that she could see her own reflected in his eyes. His nearness was like a slow, sweet poison, spreading through her, paralysing all movement.

He sensed her response and slid one hand behind her head, his fingers tangling in her hair and pulling her head back and to one side. Then he bent to lay his lips against her ear, the tip of his tongue exploring the curl of thin, smooth skin. She held her breath, fighting down the turbulence that roared through her. But her body betrayed her and she found herself leaning towards him.

His lips lingered for a moment, then moved to brush along her eyebrows, rest against her closed eyes with deceptive gentleness. Then suddenly she was pressed closely against him as he kissed her with a violence that crushed and plundered.

'Let's get out of here,' he said roughly. 'You were right—it's not my scene. Especially tonight.'

Someone changed the tape, and, as the raw, strident notes exploded through the flat, Fay felt them like blows to the solar plexus. Instantly she was wide awake, snapped back to reality.

'Come on,' he said, grasping her hand and half turning, 'I've got a place in town. Let's go!'

With a strength she didn't know she possessed, Fay dragged her hand away. 'How *dare* you?' she whispered. 'Get out! You've got it all wrong! Don't overestimate your attraction, Craig. I knew you were arrogant, but really... How can you be so thick-skinned?' She stood back, her eyes flashing, her breast heaving with fury. 'I don't know what the set-up is with you and Claudia; I don't want to know! But I *do* know that you deliberately misled me into believing that you hardly knew her—if at all. And now you have the gall to——'

'Why, you're jealous!' he breathed. Then he smiled.

It was the smile that did it, sending Fay over the top. 'How utterly, unbelievably conceited you are!' she exclaimed, loathing him. 'Why should I be jealous? You mean nothing to me. I thought I had made that clear from the beginning. I don't know what your game is, but if you thought for one moment that I was fool enough to fall for all that hackneyed——'

'And, of course,' he grated, 'your life is carefully mapped out on a nice, flat plateau in Paris.'

'I wouldn't define it quite that way, but, yes, it seems that you *have* got the message. So, in that case, why on earth should I be jealous of Claudia? Just to lay it right on the line, there's no place in my life for one-night stands with a man like you. And I bitterly regret the fact that my grandfather's legacy threw us into the same space for a while. So, as I said earlier, I'd be obliged if you would get your stuff out of Brantye *immediately*. And that is all I have—or want—to say to you. *Ever*.'

She hadn't realised that she was capable of such undiluted rage, but to her complete chagrin he threw back his head and laughed. 'How you do go on,' he murmured. 'I find it quite amazing that a high-flying career lady like yourself can go off at such a tangent, and all because of a few wrong ideas. However, in the present circumstances, I'll go. I don't particularly enjoy bandying arguments with a lady who's so wrapped up in her own safety-belt that she's unwilling to enjoy the ride. But there'll be other days when you've cooled down. I'll be back.'

His ability to meet Fay's raging frustration with an unshakeable calm maddened her to a point she had never reached before. Unseeingly her hand groped for something and found only the breadboard. She lifted her arm and flung it after him as he turned for a moment in the doorway. He fielded it neatly and spun it back so that it clattered at her feet. Then he closed the door quietly behind him, and she was left caught up in a maelstrom of emotion that seemed to churn the very marrow in her bones.

CHAPTER FIVE

CALMNESS returned the following day as Fay unfastened her safety-belt and leaned thankfully into the aeroplane seat, closing her eyes. Early in life she had learned how exhausting emotions could be, but it was years since she had felt as raw and battered as she had last night.

Her need to get back to her own life and pick up the threads amounted almost to panic, and when Vicky had tried to persuade her to stay on for another day or two she had been adamant.

'It seems to me that you can't wait to shake the dust of England off your feet,' Vicky had grumbled, as they cleaned up the flat together. 'By the way, Craig left rather abruptly, didn't he? Didn't even say goodnight to me.'

'Well, you were occupied, and I suppose he didn't want to interrupt. Anyway, he only dropped in to return something I had left at Brantye, and to bring you the little dish,' Fay had said.

'Yes, wasn't that nice of him?' Vicky had smiled, then sat back on her heels. 'From the way you two danced together, I'd say you made quite a hit.'

'Don't be silly! He's—well, he's just that kind of man...'

'Yes, I suppose so. Still——' Vicky had winked salaciously '—that kind of thing is nice while it lasts.'

It was unbearable, Fay had argued silently, stacking empty wine bottles in a box.

And now she felt as if she had been pulled through the eye of a hurricane. A feeling of unease, of being slightly out of tune with events, lingered sourly. Her decision to sell Brantye, thereby severing the last Armitage links with the old place, and breaking a pattern of two centuries, made her feel something of a traitor. Then there was her disastrous experience with Craig: fire and ice, ecstasy and anger... It didn't bear thinking about; she would put it right out of her mind. But, like a wound, it had left a scar which would take a long time to fade.

To cap it all, there was her apprehension over Claudia's intended visit. Craig Mackenzie might mock my ideas of self-preservation, Fay thought bitterly, but at least they offered security and peace.

She tried to shake off her gloom, but Claudia's remarks had left her with an uncomfortably hunted feeling.

What did Claudia want this time? Had Vicky been right about their stepmother's motives being purely mercenary? Judging by her appearance, she didn't seem short of money. That wedding outfit must have been very expensive. And Claudia had always been extravagant. Maybe, Fay thought wearily, money had been her motive for marrying into the Armitage family.

Fay tried to quell all thoughts of the past, but her brain was racing. Claudia, in her twenties, had been radiantly lovely, and when she'd first met Fay's father he couldn't have been at his best, sunk in grief as he was. And the fact that the marriage hadn't been very satisfactory seemed to confirm the idea that Claudia hadn't married for love. So if it was for financial security, that would explain a lot—like those times when Claudia had tried to persuade her husband to make his peace with old Julius. It might also explain why, despite Julius's coldness, Claudia always made a point of remembering his birthday, and of sending him a case of wine at Christmas. Julius had never acknowledged the gifts, yet still Claudia had persisted in trying to heal the rift.

If she had succeeded in reknitting family ties, Fay thought, the probe of her mind busy, then no doubt she would have benefited under Julius's will. Instead of which, apart from a few bequests, the bulk of his estate had passed to Vicky and herself—and to Craig Mackenzie, of course.

Fay shifted in her seat. She would *not* think of him! And as for his remark that he would be back... Fay's mouth twitched in derisive, silent laughter—that, too, was undoubtedly part of his approach to women.

The French coastline passed beneath them, and Fay gave herself a little shake, shrugging off such unsatisfactory thoughts. Sensibly she would leave them behind, on the other side of the Channel.

Outside her apartment lay a sheaf of red roses. Fay's face softened. Dear Christophe! How fortunate she was to have a man like him in the background. Immediately she had showered and changed she would telephone him and thank him. And perhaps tonight they would dine out somewhere, and everything would fall into place again.

Smiling, she let herself into her apartment, then flung open the windows, hearing the buzz of Paris traffic, the blare of someone's radio. A knot of tourists stood at the corner of the street, studying a map, doubtless going off to the Panthéon. There was the good smell of bread from the *boulangerie* along the street, the crooked red roofs where two pigeons preened in the sunshine... Soon, the window-boxes opposite would be ablaze with geraniums. All so familiar, so dear. And perhaps, she told herself optimistically, the last few days weren't a complete disaster, for she had come back with some ideas for a collection inspired by the dusty, damson bloom of the faded curtains of Brantye, the soft dusky rose of ancient velvet cushions... Something along medieval lines, she decided, her imagination clicking into gear.

Still smiling absently, she drew out a card from the sheaf of flowers. Not Christophe's hand-written welcome home message, but the hand of some anonymous florist, the words written in English with a spelling mistake. 'I'll be their, remember. C.'

A flare of shock soared inside her, and forcefully she thrust the roses into the rubbish bin and dusted off her hands. Red roses! she thought scornfully. How very unoriginal! He had borrowed that particular gesture from Christophe.

Christophe's pleasant voice was balm to her bruised spirits. He was an undemanding man, deeply involved in his family business, and they had what Fay thought was a perfect relationship. Her sister had described him as 'stuffy', and perhaps to someone as volatile and energetic as Vicky he did indeed seem that way. Vicky was under the impression that all Frenchmen were dangerously sexy and ardent. Fay smiled. Christophe's virtues were more worthy: he was safe, reliable and thoughtful.

Fay knew that his marriage had ended in divorce three years ago, since when, he had told her, he was 'Almost married to the bank, but not entirely.' His blue eyes had hinted that she also occupied an important place in his life, and as their comfortable relationship developed she began to sense his intentions towards her. With Christophe there would be no dizzy heights, but no abysmal depths either. With Christophe she would always know exactly where she stood. Life with him would be easy, very pleasant and extremely civilised.

As he tucked her arm into his and they went into the expensive restaurant, Fay was able to push the memory of the past days to the back of her mind in the pleasure of being with him again.

She felt relaxed and content as she tried to describe her inheritance. 'I shall sell it, of course,' she concluded with a smile. 'There's little point in holding on to it when my future is here.'

'I'm pleased to hear it.' Christophe reached for her hand, absently fondling it. 'And you must allow me to advise you about investing the money from the sale.'

'I would be grateful for that,' Fay said warmly. 'And now, what have you been doing while I was away?'

Christophe withdrew his hand as the waiter shook out Fay's napkin and spread it on her lap.

'You know perfectly well,' he smiled. 'Working—very hard, very long. And, I'm pleased to say, very successfully.' For a moment he gave his attention to the wine, sipping critically, pausing, then nodding to the *sommelier*. Then he began to speak of a business deal which he had brought to a very satisfactory conclusion, the movement of a vast sum of money, and the wisdom of his earlier manipulative tactics. He was very discreet, disclosing no secrets, breaking no confidences, but there was a complacency about him which, for no apparent reason, Fay began to find mildly irritating.

Her attention wandered, losing the thread of conversation. And out of the blue thundered the unspoken question: how does *he* feel about *other* things? About aesthetic or idealistic values—like—like—conservation, for example? Had they ever discussed such matters? She couldn't remember.

With a shock she realised that she had completely lost the vein of his story now. She must be more tired by recent events than she had thought. But she smiled and nodded, and as he talked she watched him. Dark, smooth hair, receding slightly, a tinge of blueness to his jaw which in a different kind of man might have passed for 'designer stubble' and wasn't unattractive. His manners were beautiful, urbane, polished; he was always in control. Yes, altogether Christophe was a very attractive man. And yet, a tiny inner voice persisted, wasn't there something lacking? Fire and force, and some magic ingredient that could infuse a moment with—excitement? Crossly she caught herself up. She had had enough of those back in England, hadn't she?

Christophe finished his story and looked at her fondly. 'I'm so happy to have you back,' he said softly, his blue eyes gentle. 'Paris is not the same without you.'

Fay smiled across at him. 'Not so happy as I am to be here,' she murmured. Who would imagine that in Paris, of all places, she had consciously felt herself unwinding? The thought struck her as amusing, and she laughed.

'There is a joke?' Christophe smiled encouragingly.

'No, not really.' She swallowed suddenly—far from a joke, more a kind of madness. All behind her now, thank heaven.

'You're not eating very much, *chérie*,' Christophe remarked. 'The meal is not to your liking, perhaps?'

'It's perfect, Christophe. I'm—not very hungry, I suppose.'

'Then shall we leave? We could dance...? Would you like that?'

Fay touched his hand lightly. 'Considerate, as always,' she murmured. 'No. I think... Would you mind if I went home?'

He pouted a little. 'I had hoped that... And I have to go away for a week or so. But——' he shrugged '—if you wish to leave...'

Quickly he settled the bill, taking Fay's arm protectively as they walked back to his car.

When they reached her apartment she didn't this time ask him up for a last drink together. She was puzzled by her own behaviour. It was due, she decided, to tiredness, the emotional strain of the past days. 'I'm sorry, Christophe,' she murmured, 'but I'm so tired.'

Instantly he understood. He kissed her drily, pleasantly, thanking her for her company. 'Goodnight, my darling, sleep well. I will call you when I get back.'

'Well! Your little holiday didn't do you much good!' Giselle remarked, the following morning.

Fay looked around the office which she shared with four other girls on the design team. She had cleared her desk before she left, but now it was littered with papers, sketches, stacks of old magazines, a dish holding pebbles in all shades of brown, and a few yarn samples. It was all so familiar, from the wizened cactus on the window-sill to the dress rails bowed under their burden of garments.

'I know,' she sighed. 'I do feel rather washed out.'

'A man?' Giselle pounced gleefully. 'Was there a man in England?' Then she laughed triumphantly. 'There was!' She turned to a thin, shaggily coiffured girl who had just come in and was throwing off a denim jacket. 'Did you hear, Natalya? I was right. Fay is blushing.'

'If my face is red,' Fay said with dignity, 'it's because it's so hot in here.' She lifted the magazines from her desk and dumped them on the floor. 'Anything exciting happen while I was away?'

'Marie and Suzi have gone to Hong Kong with two of the merchandisers ... Apart from that, nothing. Why didn't they send me?' Giselle complained. 'I never get the best trips.' She picked up a pen, examined it, then threw it down disgustedly.

Fay grinned. 'Now I *know* I'm back in harness,' she murmured. 'When I hear your early morning grumbles everything falls right back into place.' Determinedly she spread out a sheet of graph paper and hunted for the black pen she preferred to work with.

But, on second thoughts, it seemed that it might take a little time for *everything* to fall right back into place again. And she knew the reason why. Despite her intention to forget that Craig Mackenzie ever existed, somehow the—the—*essence* of the man lingered. Even during last night's meal with Christophe, thoughts of Craig had intruded. And that was all wrong. Yet even the fact that Christophe seemed to be working towards marriage hadn't successfully ousted the totally unwelcome memories that she had brought back from Sussex. And last night she had dreamed about Craig, too. Disjointed, incomprehensible images and events. How that would feed his ego if he knew! she thought bitterly. Especially as he seemed to be having some kind of affair with Claudia—not that it had prevented him from amusing himself in Claudia's absence.

And Claudia... Fay's stomach contracted uneasily. If her stepmother intended paying her a visit, then the sooner she got it over with, the better! Fay crumpled the sheet of paper and hurled it into the bin. Human relationships could be hell at times!

But by eleven o'clock her job had taken over, thankfully clearing her mind of all other matters, and when Giselle suggested that they go to a pizza parlour for lunch Fay agreed, surprised by the swift passage of time, and grateful for her friend's light-hearted company.

Fay worked late that night, and when she got back to her apartment she took a quick bath, ate a light supper and went straight to bed, telling herself that each day would bring her back a little closer to the peace of mind she had once known and now longed for. Some time she must write to Mr Seymour and ask him to put Brantye into the hands of an estate agent, but that could wait for a few weeks. It would give Craig time to get his furniture out; common sense told her that she must avoid any further direct communication with him.

For a moment a raw ache stirred in a secret cell of her heart, but resolutely she squashed it.

The week passed uneventfully with still no message from Claudia, and Fay tried hard not to wonder what Claudia and Craig might be doing together.

When Fay's doorbell rang on Sunday morning she heard it with misgivings. Hastily she put away the last of her food shopping and whipped a comb through her hair. It was vitally important to greet Claudia with at least a little confidence in her appearance. Claudia had a disconcerting way of missing nothing, from a laddered stocking to a broken fingernail, and under her apparently gentle scrutiny such small defects could assume gigantic and unnerving proportions.

Lifting her head and fastening a bright smile on her face, Fay flung open the door. And was suddenly dizzy. Craig was standing there, smiling blandly.

'Hello, Fay.' His voice was as smooth as his expression.

The nerves in Fay's stomach leaped as she gazed wide-eyed at him.

He looked beyond her to the open living-room door at the end of the narrow hall. 'May I come in?' But already he was past her.

Fay stood paralysed, her mind in a spin. He was the very last person she'd expected to see. Despite his earlier promise that they would meet again in Paris, enough had happened since then to cancel absolutely that idea! She bit her lip. What a nerve he had!

'I expect you're surprised to see me,' he said evenly. 'I mentioned that I would be coming over in a couple of weeks, but something cropped up earlier than I anticipated. So, as you see, here I am.' He spread his arms with that lithe, fluid movement which was one of the things about him that Fay had been unable to scrub from her memory. 'And I do believe I smell coffee.' He smiled easily. 'You must be psychic.'

'If I were psychic, I wouldn't have opened the door,' Fay said stonily, her narrowed eyes glinting green.

But Craig didn't appear to have heard. He stood looking around, perfectly at ease and apparently unaware of Fay's inner tumult. 'How pleasant,' he approved, 'and more or less as I might have imagined it.' Then he faced her. 'But it looks as if you didn't get my flowers.'

Fay gave a dry swallow, then nodded. Her face felt stiff, but every nerve-end in her body tingled, partly through anger, but mostly because of his presence, which seemed to fill the room disturbingly. Hastily she moved away from him, then finding her voice again she said coldly, 'Your flowers—yes, I got them.'

'Oh?' The dark, mobile eyebrows flicked up questioningly. 'I assumed that you like red roses.'

'I do.'

'But... You—threw them out?' The imperturbable smile broadened infuriatingly. 'I'm right, aren't I?' He laughed. 'What a grand, prima-donna gesture. You must have enjoyed it!'

'I did,' she said coldly.

'I see.' He paused, his eyes narrowing fractionally as he watched her. 'So I take it that it wasn't the flowers you disliked. Just the sender.'

'You could say that. What did you expect?'

He shrugged, focusing Fay's gaze on the broad, tweed-clad shoulders. 'A good question. I'm never quite sure just what to expect from you.'

With an effort Fay glanced away. It was like trying to break up a magnetic field, she thought miserably, for his face, eyes, mouth, even the shape of his head with that luxuriant black hair and closely set ears seemed to exercise a pull on her gaze as forceful as gravity.

'Don't tell me,' she murmured scathingly, 'that Craig Mackenzie is actually at a loss, for once. As for your expectations, forget them. You can expect nothing from me.'

She was deliberately trying to provoke him into leaving. Why couldn't he realise that he was unwelcome here and leave her in peace? Let him go back to Claudia, where she was sure that he would get a much warmer welcome.

But his impatient frown dismissed her retort. 'Look,' he said spikily, 'instead of standing here like opponents sizing each other up in the ring, why don't we sit down and talk? And a cup of that coffee wouldn't come amiss. Or doesn't your generosity extend that far?'

'Oh, you may have a cup of coffee,' Fay said indifferently, 'if that's *all* you want.'

'Don't bank on it,' he answered, but so softly that she wasn't absolutely sure she heard him correctly.

She was glad to escape, and for a moment she stood by the cooker drawing deep, slow breaths, but her hands trembled a little as she laid a tray. She felt shaken all the way through. Really, she thought incoherently, after hurling that breadboard... And after his suggestion that they go back to his place... Utterly beyond belief that he would have the—effrontery to turn up here... Anyway, how had he known her address? Oh, of course, he would have phoned Vicky. Yes, that would be it. He must have called her on the day that Fay flew back to Paris. Otherwise, how would he have known where to send the roses? She had been too angry and wound up to give that a thought at the time.

As she set down the tray on a low table she voiced the question.

'Oh, it was simple,' he answered. 'Like the neat and well-organised lady you are, you had a clearly marked label in a little transparent case attached to the handle of your luggage. I carried it in at Brantye, if you recall. And I happen to have a good memory for such things.' He watched her over his cup, steadily and disturbingly. 'I also remember an afternoon up on the Downs,' he said silkily. 'And then, later, outside the gate of Brantye. Don't you? Don't *you*, Fay?' he repeated with persuasive softness.

'Not very clearly.' She injected a note of indifference into her voice. 'I soon forget things I don't *wish* to remember.' She sat back, smoothing her skirt.

'Liar.' He spoke softly, almost as if the word were an endearment. Then, more briskly, with a taunting light in his dark eyes, 'So we're still trying to cling to the virtues of a passive, pedestrian lifestyle, are we? Still afraid to face facts, to dig below the surface?'

Fay frowned. 'As I've told you before, my lifestyle is my own affair,' she snapped.

'Well, perhaps... But it looked to me that, for a little while, you ventured into water rather deeper than usual. And, more important, you actually enjoyed it. Although, of course, you won't admit it because that would make a nonsense of your comfortable, conventional values.' He lifted a warning hand. 'And please don't tell me I'm arrogant or conceited or any of the other flattering epithets you used previously.

'I won't,' Fay said quickly. 'You know that already. Now, I'm getting tired of this conversation. So why *did* you come?' She eyed him dispassionately.

'Well,' he murmured placatingly, 'I decided to put that last little incident down to the heat of the moment. And by the way, your aim with a breadboard is pretty good.

And I told myself that, with a nice, quiet girl like you, that little display of temper was right out of character. So now I'm giving you the opportunity to make amends.'

'Why—you . . . I don't know how you have the nerve! You... I... *Oh!*' Words choked her as rage ticked inside like a time bomb ready to explode. 'I've never met anyone so—so utterly insufferable.' She tightened her mouth, jerking away to glare unseeingly out of the window.

'All right,' he said laconically, 'you needn't blow a fuse. I get your drift.' Then, surprisingly, he laughed. 'Come on, Fay, I was joking. You shouldn't be so sensitive. If you want the truth, I'm at a loose end today, and I thought I might take you out somewhere. Just to show that I bear no malice,' he went on smoothly. 'That is, of course, if your boyfriend hasn't beaten me to it.'

'If you must know,' she said coolly, 'he's away at the moment.'

'His loss,' Craig commented. 'And my gain, perhaps?' When she didn't answer he said, 'Come on, Fay. What about it? If you have nothing special to do today, then let's do it together. But peaceably, I hope. Think you can manage that?'

Fay glowered at him for a moment, then busied herself refilling their cups. But he took the coffee-pot from her. For a second their fingers brushed. Instantly the thrill flared through her, obliterating everything else, even her resentment. He set the pot down. 'No more for me, thank you.'

Fay got up. She felt strained and jumpy, yet undeniably excited. Earlier she had forced herself to reject the idea that she wanted to see him again. And she badly needed the strength to send him away, right out of her life, once and for all. He was too disruptive. Over the years she had learned to handle herself—or so she had thought. But she certainly hadn't learned to handle such a wild, vivid longing as this . . . How could she have, she asked herself desperately, when nothing like this had ever arisen before? And what was it about this man that, in so short a time, he could have such a shattering effect upon her composure?

She glanced at him quickly. He, too, had risen and was watching her as if he could now see the battle going on inside her. A slight smile tilted his mouth, softening the harsh, almost brutal jawline, but his eyes held a challenge, daring her, compelling her . . . 'Well,' she said briskly, 'I can't suddenly invent a previous engagement. And I'm not particularly busy—at least not with anything that can't wait.' She glanced at her watch. 'So, all right. I might as well accept. I'll get my coat.'

Certainly her voice hadn't betrayed the confusion of her thoughts. But her bedroom mirror reflected a face still lit with the last vestiges of anger, and her eyes sparkled, grey-green, with a shy, wary uncertainty. Her fingers fluttered slightly as she clipped on jade earrings that matched the stripes of her silk shirt, but their tremor was nothing compared with the vibrations that seemed to be going on inside her.

With something of a losing gambler's bravado, she knotted a green silk scarf around her neck, slung on her shoulder-bag and walked erectly back into the living-room.

'Ready now?' Craig's eyes approved the soft white wool jacket. 'Then let's go? Where to?'

'Honfleur,' Fay returned promptly.

He laughed. 'I had anticipated somewhere more local. Why Honfleur?'

Why indeed? Fay wondered. The name had sprung to her lips without conscious deliberation. But perhaps that, too, was part and parcel of this strange morning. 'Simply because I like the place. Isn't that enough? Or were you anticipating a conducted tour around the Paris sewers?'

His mouth quirked. 'Nothing so off-beat, particularly with you dressed like that. All right, then, Honfleur it is.'

Fay's sense of elation climbed as they sped along the busy motorway towards the coast. She felt intoxicated. A glow of freedom, of having thrown off self-imposed shackles suffused her. Who would have thought, she wondered, that only two hours ago I was wondering how to fill the day? But then, who would have thought that Craig would turn up out of the blue like that? The only thing she *was* sure of was that he was responsible for the way she was now feeling.

She sneaked a glance at the strong, rather sombre profile. You don't know him, she told herself sternly, trying to settle the clamour inside herself. You're not even sure that you want to. And *he's* only here because he has nothing better to do. He's admitted that. And, anyway, there was something between him and Claudia, and Fay had never yet found anything in common with any of her stepmother's friends.

Craig's voice interrupted her thoughts as he overtook one of the giant lorries thundering towards Le Havre. 'What have you been doing with yourself since you got back?'

'Working hard, of course. Oh, I did dine out one night at a very luxurious place.'

'Only—*one* night?'

'I told you,' she replied calmly, 'that Christophe had to go away.'

'Ah, yes. Then here's to Christophe,' Craig said sardonically. 'Is he as distinguished as his name suggests?'

'*I* think so,' Fay murmured.

'And *I* think I'd prefer to talk about your work instead. So you've been kept busy?'

'Mmm.' She went on to speak of the summer collection she was involved in. 'Not this coming summer, naturally,' she enlarged. 'We work well in advance.'

'That must require a great degree of confidence in the future,' he remarked idly.

'That's the way it goes.'

He changed gear, double-declutching smoothly to suit the gearbox. Fay sensed the play of his leg muscles and looked away quickly. 'Tell me, Fay, doesn't that give you a sense of power?' he mocked. 'Knowing so far ahead what women will be wearing?'

'Of course,' she dismissed airily. 'I'm dizzy with power. Women will be wearing what we tell 'em.' She laughed.

He gave a reverent whistle. 'Fay the omnipotent! So who's arrogant now?'

She laughed again, tilting her head back, and saw him flick a disturbing, oblique glance at the curve of her throat. Something warm inside her expanded deliciously. She suppressed it after a moment, managing to hold on to the mood of banter between them. 'Oh, come on,' she protested, 'I'm sure *you* have a stake in the future, too. Don't you keep your nose to the ground, trying to pick up any little scents which promise that some obscure artist is suddenly going up in the popularity stakes? And so the value of his work will increase?'

He nodded, grinning. 'As we're in France,' he said, '*touché.*' Then he went on thoughtfully, 'You're different today. Less taut and hung-up. I like it. I like it very much. A distinct improvement on our last meeting, wouldn't you say? Although I loved your dress.'

'Did you?' she asked in a muffled voice. She stared at his hands on the wheel, shapely, with a strong competence to them that was at variance with most people's ideas of an artist's hands. These hands looked as if they could control a stallion, lift a *tonne*, yet cradle and caress... She caught her breath and looked away quickly. Awareness of every living cell under her own skin made her equally conscious of the closeness of his body. She had known the strength in those arms, the touch of that sensuous mouth, the intimate search of his tongue. Panic swelled suddenly. Just supposing, a sly little inner voice asked, just supposing you had taken him up on that invitation at Vicky's that evening, and gone back with him to his London house? How would it have been—in his arms, close to his naked body...? Her eyes snapped wide open and she sat bolt upright in the seat. For heaven's sake, stop it! she ranted inwardly. But the sneaky little voice persisted. Indescribable? it suggested. Unbearable! her common sense snapped.

She cleared her throat, and, trying to recapture the casual mood, asked him why he had come to Paris.

'Just to give an informed opinion,' he said. 'But unfortunately I had to disappoint my client. I don't relish telling a man who thinks he's got a fortune hanging on his wall that the dark squiggle in the corner of the canvas, mixed up with the heather and the rocks, isn't simply a master's brushstroke but the signature of a gifted amateur. And, you know, the last century bred a host of very talented amateurs, particularly among the women. Some of their water-colours are exquisite. But if it's not the real thing, then——' he shrugged, his arm touching hers for a moment '—there is little real value.'

At the waterside café in Honfleur Fay asked for a *Kir*, but Craig said quickly to the waiter, 'Make that a *Kir Royale*.'

Fay's eyebrows arched. 'Isn't that a little extravagant?' she murmured. 'Cassis and white wine is good enough for me.'

'Today it will be cassis and champagne,' he said firmly. 'I think I can say,' he went on musingly, 'without undue conceit, that I treat my women well.'

He was joking, of course, Fay told herself, but a sudden picture of him with Claudia flashed before her. 'Besides,' he went on, 'this is a champagne day. Even the sun is coming out for us.'

Determinedly Fay shut out the images of Craig and Claudia together. 'This is one of my favourite places,' she remarked.

'Then perhaps I should feel flattered that you chose to bring me here,' he murmured.

To their left the tall, narrow, slate-hung buildings looked as if they could withstand all change and still maintain their architectural integrity. 'Kind of—arrogant,' Fay mused aloud. Then, catching Craig's sardonic glance, 'Oh, not you, *this* time,' she said calmly. 'Nor me. I'm talking about the buildings. It's as if they know they're exactly right for this place just as they are. Trippers and yachtsmen and fishermen and artists will come and go, but they don't care.' The harbour and the boats were bathed in a pale primrose light that silvered the grey water. 'Misty, watery, magical,' she said softly. 'No wonder the painters came in their never-ceasing quest for qualities of light.'

'You don't have to talk art just to please *me*,' Craig quipped.

'I can't think what gave you the idea that I was. Don't you know me better than that?' She laughed.

Craig looked at her and seemed about to say something when the waiter brought their *poulet Vallée d'Auge*.

'Maybe some of the artists came for the food, too,' he suggested, grinning, as he picked up his fork.

'What a prosaic thought—and from a man whose field is art,' Fay teased.

'Well, as art pays for my bread and butter it was a valid observation,' he argued. 'Besides, today I'm on holiday in a country where food, among other things, is important. Does what's his-name—Christophe?—bring you here?' he asked suddenly.

'No.' Fay concentrated on the chicken in its creamy sauce. Honfleur wasn't Christophe's kind of place. Ten minutes here would be enough for him.

'So what do you usually do on Sundays? I suppose you spend the day together?'

'Rarely. You see, there's a long-standing tradition in Christophe's family that the clan gathers for their Sunday midday meal.'

Fay had been invited four Sundays ago. Christophe's three older brothers, with their wives and amazingly sophisticated teenage children had been there, along with uncles and cousins whose exact relationship Fay hadn't managed to establish. Christophe's mother, regal in rustling grey silk, had been gracious but rather distant. To Fay, the meal had seemed unnecessarily elaborate. Her own idea of family lunch parties dated back to her mother's time, when tureens of soup, a buffet table and a comprehensive fresh fruit salad had been displayed. People helped themselves, sitting where they liked and moving into a different group when they wished.

But the Lefèvre family didn't do things that way. At the end of the long meal Fay had managed to signal to Christophe that she had a headache, and thankfully he'd taken her into the garden. It had seemed just as formal as the house. Christophe's father had joined them and said something charming about 'an English rose in a

French garden.' Afterwards Christophe had kissed her restrainedly behind the gazebo. 'You were a success,' he'd told her, smiling. And Fay had repressed a sudden urge to ask what had he expected? That she might use the wrong cutlery?

When she married Christophe—*if* she married him, she amended hastily—she would be part of that Sunday lunchtime tradition.

'Come back.' Craig's voice cut through her reflections. 'You were miles away.'

'Yes, I was.' Fay laughed apologetically. Compared with that Sunday in Paris, this seemed like a carnival. As she met Craig's quizzical stare, she looked down quickly, blushing for no apparent reason.

Suddenly, before she realised what he was doing, he reached across, took her hand and raised it to his lips. 'Just another little French mannerism I've picked up,' he murmured urbanely. 'You were looking adorably guilty.'

'Well,' she protested, trying to take a hold on herself, 'I can't think where you got that idea. And, just for the record, no Frenchman has ever kissed my hand.'

'Then you haven't lived.' He grinned. 'But I think I've said that before. What about the boyfriend? Oh, all right,' he added crisply, 'perhaps I shouldn't have asked.'

'No,' Fay answered coolly, 'you shouldn't.'

At a stroke the need to draw back from him was reinforced. Whatever she felt like inside, she must fight the undertow that seemed to be pulling her inexorably closer to him by the minute. But there was one sure way of dealing with it. 'By the way, how's Claudia?' she asked carelessly.

Craig's face was carefully blank. 'Fine, the last time I saw her. Why bring her name up?'

'No reason particularly,' Fay shrugged vaguely. 'It was just that when I saw you standing at my front door my immediate thought was that you had brought a message from her.' She glanced up at the waiter. 'I'll have the *rhum baba*,' she said, as if the subject of Claudia was now closed.

'For me, too,' Craig murmured impatiently. Then he leaned his forearms on the table and regarded Fay sternly. 'I am not Claudia's messenger boy,' he clipped out. 'I don't run her errands. But obviously you're not convinced. You know, Fay,' he went on, his gaze narrowing, 'you really must resist the temptation to jump to conclusions that have no basis in fact.'

She flushed angrily, staring at him, her eyes stormy, her mouth set obstinately. Who was he to tell her what she must and must not do? 'Your relationship with my stepmother isn't of any interest to me,' she said indifferently. 'But don't forget, I did see the way she greeted you at Brantye, and the way you seemed very——'

'Oh? You want to talk about Claudia, do you?' he said sharply. 'All right, then. But for something that's of no interest to you, you seem remarkably curious. Right, then, we'll talk about her.'

Fay shook her head emphatically, the thick, red-gold curls dancing wildly, catching the sunlight. 'I don't want to talk about her. I merely asked how she was.'

'Do you really want to know? Do you care?' he added cruelly.

Fay bit her lip. This was what she had wanted to achieve, wasn't it? This widening chasm?

'However,' Craig went on, 'as you raised the subject——'

'You didn't seem so eager to talk about her that night over steak in The Feathers,' Fay murmured coldly. 'You led me on, letting me confide in you, tell you things about my relationship with her, yet you never even mentioned that you knew her.'

'Ah!' Craig exclaimed with satisfaction. 'So that rankles, does it?'

'Not particularly. Although surely even *you* must realise that it seemed rather odd. Now, shall we go?' She stood up, but Craig reached out, his fingers closing around her arm as he pulled her down into her seat again.

'Sit down,' he gritted. 'I haven't finished. You seem to think I owe you an explanation. All right, then shut up and you shall have it. No, I didn't mention that I knew Claudia, but not out of any desire to deliberately deceive you. By the time you were talking about her it was too late; I felt it might embarrass you to learn that I knew her. That's all. I wasn't trying to conceal anything. Got that?'

Fay stared at him stonily. When she didn't answer he went on, 'When I realised that you and Claudia weren't the firm friends she had led me to suppose, there was little I could say, anyway. You don't like her much, that's clear. But I don't have your reasons for disliking her, so I see her differently. That's natural, isn't it?' he barked.

'Oh, perfectly,' Fay said sweetly. 'You're a man, and she's very attractive.'

'Must you state the obvious?'

'Oh, heavens,' Fay sighed, 'I merely asked how she was. Now, can we drop the subject?' It had achieved its purpose, she thought, as she saw the impatient flicker of anger in Craig's eyes, the tightening of his jaw. She glanced at her watch. 'I ought to get back,' she said.

'Not until I've finished. What's wrong with you, Fay, that you deliberately set out to spoil what could have been a very pleasant day?'

'I don't know what you're talking about,' she snapped. 'And I wish you'd stop—hectoring me.'

Craig hesitated for a moment, then threw down a few notes on the dish that held the bill and stood up. 'Very well, we'll go. With you in your present mood there's no point in staying.'

Fay had to run to keep up with him as he strode to the car. Inside she felt empty, drained. But it was for the best. She had been a fool to come. She'd known that at the time, but that reckless feeling had gained the upper hand temporarily. Now she reminded herself yet again of Craig's initial dislike, of his utter nerve in asking her to go back with him to his London house. And all the time he was playing Claudia along. Certainly Claudia seemed to be eating out of his hand that afternoon at Brantye, perfectly at ease with him and looking forward to their dinner date. He probably had plenty of other girlfriends as well... Unfortunately he was unforgettably attractive—and secretive with it!

If I hadn't come with him today, she thought, as she got into the car, I would have spent the afternoon wishing I had. And now I regret that I did!

'Right,' Craig said briskly as they left the little town behind, 'I'm going to put you in the picture about a few things. I first met Claudia——'

'I don't want to know,' Fay muttered. 'I don't——'

'Shut up,' he growled. 'What's so special about you that you must be shielded from the truth?'

'I've no idea what you're talking about,' she said icily.

'No, you haven't. So I'll tell you. As I was saying, I first met Claudia some years ago, after your father died. She came to Brantye to see Julius.'

Fay sat up straight. 'I don't believe you,' she snapped. 'Grandfather would have nothing to do with her. Anyway, if she had, then I would have known about it.'

'Well, in this case it seems that you *didn't* know. You had gone back to college. Claudia came to ask for a loan—something to do with a boutique, or some such thing.'

Fay tensed, prepared now to listen.

'Julius gave her the money—quite a substantial sum. A year or so later she was back.'

Fay swallowed. Then she said in a small voice, 'The boutique failed.' Then, after a moment, 'I find it hard to believe that Grandfather even entertained her. He disliked her intensely.'

'Well, as she was his widowed daughter-in-law perhaps he felt he had some responsibility towards her. Also he thought it would benefit you and Vicky. So,' Craig went on cruelly, 'you can see that Julius wasn't quite the ogre you believed him to be. You probably didn't know, either, that he contributed generously to your support—yours and Vicky's? No? Of course, it was all done through Jeff Seymour, his solicitor.'

'You're enjoying this, aren't you?' Fay breathed. 'Whatever you say, you resent my having Brantye. And now you're trying to make me feel bad again about not going to see Grandfather, not going to the funeral, not playing the devoted granddaughter when, in fact, he was so generous. That's it, isn't it?'

'Conscience pricking you?' Craig said acidly. 'I'm telling you all this simply to explain how I came to know Claudia. As for Julius—no, he didn't like her, but he was prepared to help her when he thought she was making an attempt to stand on her own two feet.'

'Well, I didn't know anything about it,' Fay said doggedly.

'Then, when Claudia came back a second time, Julius would have nothing to do with her for a while. Afterwards he relented and made some provision for her. That, of course, ceased at his death.'

'But my father left money——'

'Not enough, apparently,' Craig said drily.

Fay stared out of the window for a while, then she said in a muffled voice, 'Well, are you satisfied now? You've succeeded in making me feel thoroughly guilty about Grandfather. You also make me—ashamed that you know so much more about my own family than I do.'

'I repeat,' Craig said in steely tones, 'I'm simply telling you this to explain how I came to meet Claudia. After Julius's funeral she came to see me. She was friendly and charming and very pleasant company.'

Fay nodded. She would be. Claudia could be excellent company at times, making it easy to forget her other side until some small incident brought it to the surface again.

'Besides,' Craig went on, 'I had a sneaking feeling that Julius had been rather unreasonable about her marriage to your father. He didn't give her much of a chance. As you know, he could be an awkward cuss when he wanted. So perhaps she sensed that I was slightly sympathetic towards her. Anyway, after his death I was glad of her company. I missed him. Despite the age difference, he was my closest friend. Claudia helped to take my mind off things.'

Fay slid a covert glance over his face, silenced by his simple statement. Despite the unemotional tone, she sensed the grief behind the proud, closed features.

'And that's all,' he resumed. 'Now do you believe me?'

Still Fay hesitated. Then she nodded reluctantly. 'I'm beginning to,' she murmured.

'Good. That's a start.'

When they reached her flat, he said abruptly, 'I could use a cup of coffee before I head back to Calais, particularly as you were in such a hurry to get up from the lunch table.'

For a moment Fay toyed with a refusal. She felt emotionally tattered.

'But of course,' he went on in an expressionless voice, noting her hesitation, 'I wouldn't dream of putting you to any trouble.'

'It's no trouble,' she said tightly at last, unlocking her flat door.

The sky was overcast with a threatening storm, and the hall was dark. She put out her hand towards the light switch. 'Don't do that,' he said quickly.

'Why on earth not?' Her words were pitched too high. She felt a sense of dislocation brought about by the see-saw of the day's emotions. She reached out to the wall again, but Craig covered the switch with his hand. Her fingers touched his skin and recoiled as if stung.

'Don't ask stupid questions,' he growled.

'Look, Craig, I really——'

But her protest was sealed behind her lips as his mouth found hers. In the same moment she found herself in his arms, her senses leaping in response to his touch as if they had been waiting for this very moment.

His lips were dry with a heat that scorched her. His hands raked roughly through her hair. The last grains of logic drained away like sand in an hourglass. She stifled her little moan of despair as he pulled her to him more closely, dominating her completely. And then she knew that in spite of everything this was all she wanted: his hands on her body, her hips ground against his, her breast suffused by the ecstatic pain of the pressure of his broad chest.

She felt him tense suddenly. Then he pushed her away. 'Forget that coffee,' he said through tight lips. 'Save it for another time. I've just remembered something. I'd better go.'

She watched him open the door and close it behind him. She shook her head slowly, her body still aching for him, her mind refusing to accept his abrupt departure. Then, with a painful sense of anticlimax, she went into the bedroom to take off her coat.

CHAPTER SIX

WITH a strange sense of relief Fay settled down at her desk the following morning. Her feelings about the previous day were curiously mixed, her thoughts at odds with each other. On the one hand, Craig had seemed sufficiently interested to pursue their earlier tentative arrangement in spite of that stormy scene at Vicky's party. But on the other hand, by his own admission, he had found himself at a loose end in Paris, so the two facts seemed to cancel each other out, leaving Fay none the wiser about his true motives.

During those hours in Honfleur there had been some rather nice moments, she thought wistfully, resisting an impulse to relive them. Yet the old hostility had lain, just below the surface, ready to spark at the slightest provocation.

And, finally, there was that kiss: rough, forceful, importunate. But *brief*—because he had suddenly remembered something he had to do, or some place where he should be! That certainly put her in her place!

Impatiently Fay leafed through some sketches without really seeing them. It was pointless trying to define the reasons that might lie behind Craig's behaviour; he was as secretive as a sealed book. As for her own feelings, she thought with a sigh, they defied understanding one way or another.

Christophe had taken a severe chill while on his business trip and was confined to bed. Fay went to visit him during the week, adding her gifts of flowers and fruit to the others which brightened his rather gloomy room.

Their conversation was stilted and unnatural, punctuated by visits from his mother and his secretary. Christophe wouldn't allow Fay to get too near to him in case she, too, picked up the bug. He was being considerate as usual, she reflected as she left, but she had wanted him to throw caution to the winds and hold out his arms to her. She desperately needed some kind of reassurance from him, some sweeping emotional gesture. In other words, she told herself wryly, I wanted him to behave completely out of character. She sighed. Her affair with Christophe seemed to be taking a downturn. Yet he hadn't changed. But *she* had, she realised sinkingly.

But at least there was some respite from the torment of her thoughts in a job offering so much stimulation, demanding such a degree of concentration that it left little energy for unsatisfactory speculation. In fact, this particular week it left little time for anything other than the demanding schedule of the summer collection, and it was with a feeling of exhausted achievement that Fay fell into bed on Friday night after long working days of sustained effort.

She awoke late on Saturday morning to sunshine streaming in through her bedroom window. Quickly she showered and was sitting by the open french windows drinking her first coffee when the doorbell rang. She frowned. Surely it couldn't be Etienne, wanting the design team to work through Saturday? It wouldn't be the first time! But no, she realised, Etienne would have telephoned, surely. Claudia, then? Maybe. Still frowning, Fay went reluctantly into the hall and opened the door. To Craig.

'Well, hello,' she faltered. 'You're certainly unpredictable.' She stepped back after a moment to let him in. His appearance whipped her thoughts into an unwelcome turmoil.

'The early hour, you mean?' His gaze drifted lazily over her tightly belted yellow housecoat. 'But I didn't specify exactly what time or date I would be collecting that coffee, did I?'

'A long time ago someone invented a device known as the telephone,' she said over her shoulder as she went into the kitchen to get another cup. 'Perhaps it would have been better to give me a little warning.'

'Warning? I don't like the word.' He leaned in the doorway, watching her. 'That suggests something sinister. Perhaps—*notice* would have been a better choice.'

'The last thing I need just now is a lecture on the use of the English language,' Fay said with some asperity. 'But all right, then, I would have appreciated a little notice. I might have been doing... Well, anything——'

She had to pass him as she went into the other room, almost brushing against him when he didn't move.

'And what visions *that* conjures up,' he drawled. He put out a hand to pick up thc cnd of thc satin sash, letting it run sensuously through his fingers. 'Nice,' he murmured. 'It suits you beautifully.' He followed her then and sat down facing her. 'Actually, this was a spur of the moment idea. I've been in Lyons for a couple of days on business, and I decided to break my journey on the flight home. I had some shopping to do in Paris, among other things.' He smiled, but there was a watchful glint in his eyes as he took the cup from her. 'Those other things depending upon how you're fixed today—that is, until my flight leaves for Heathrow.'

'My, you certainly do get about,' Fay said admiringly. 'I had no idea that you came to France so frequently.'

'Just one of those things,' he replied. 'I may not come for months, then a few things crop up more or less simultaneously. It's the way it goes. Well? How *are* you fixed today? If you're busy you only have to say the word, and I'll be off.'

He drank his coffee quickly and put the cup on the table, looking as if he was ready to leave at any moment.

Fay watched him covertly from beneath her lashes. Her heart was quickening into a timorous excitement. Now that she had got used to the idea of his being here, she didn't want to think of him leaving. Yet she rather resented the way he seemed to be using her, just turning up right out of the blue and apparently taking it for granted that she would drop everything... No, she rebuked herself, that was unfair; he *had* offered her an escape route. She had only to say that she was tied up today, and he would go. And after he had left the day would settle back into the normal Saturday routine of shopping, chores, lunch at a brasserie somewhere, and maybe a visit to an exhibition, a quick call on Christophe which his mother wouldn't welcome, although she would be too polite to say so. Or perhaps Giselle might phone, suggesting they went to a cinema. All of which had been pleasant enough once, but didn't seem such an inviting alternative now.

'No,' she said slowly, 'I'm not doing anything special today.'

'Then we'll do Paris,' he said decisively. 'So go and get dressed.'

He was an untiring companion, Fay discovered, his interest and curiosity leading them over the Seine bridges or in and out of the Métro stations, with Craig pointing out features which she had never noticed before.

Together they hunted for the graves of Sarah Bernhardt and Oscar Wilde, Peter Abelard and his Héloise. They marvelled over paintings, and Fay felt her horizons extend as he talked knowledgeably and interestingly—and often humorously—about the artists. He insisted on sampling a *croque-monsieur* in a dark little café where thirst drove Fay into drinking beer wryly, with an expression that made him laugh.

'I think,' he said at last, 'that we've done enough for one day. The rest will keep.'

They made their way back to the Left Bank, Fay footsore and exhausted, but happier than she had been for weeks. She had always loved Paris, but never so much as today, when Craig had seemed so eager to share it with her. She was about to invite him up to her apartment for supper when he glanced at his watch and said, 'Good heavens, the time! A last drink at the Deux Magots, then I must be off.'

Fay hid her disappointment as he summoned a taxi. He had become brisk and businesslike, his mind obviously already on other matters. It was as if he had already left, she thought dolefully.

'I'll drop you off at your place, then carry straight on to the airport,' he said. When the car pulled up outside her block, Craig got out to hold the door open for her, gave her hand a swift pressure and was gone.

Disconsolately she let herself in. Well, what had she expected? She smiled ruefully as she kicked off her shoes. The silence of her apartment seemed to press down on her.

Today she had been more at ease with Craig than at any time in England. Yet there had been something missing, she thought. That spark of awareness that had previously lit his eyes, just occasionally, seemed to have been lost. It made things that much more comfortable between them, and yet...

Still, she reminded herself sharply, it was what she had once wanted. She had never given him any encouragement—quite the reverse, in fact. So she couldn't really complain that he now seemed to see her simply as a useful contact in Paris who could show him the sights. And it might never happen again if his work didn't bring him back.

But two weeks later he was there again. Her heart tipped crazily when she saw him, quickening her pulses, bringing an excited light into her eyes. He had come back! He must, therefore, have thought about her while he was in England, or he wouldn't be here!

But her pulse-rate steadied when he explained that business was his reason for coming, something to do with the restoration of a small painting. She wished she could believe that that was an excuse, but she recognised it as a vain hope when he propped a stout canvas portfolio against the wall, explaining that he hadn't wanted to leave it in the car.

'No, of course not,' she agreed brightly, turning away so that he shouldn't see her disappointment.

As before, they explored Paris, looking at buildings where famous people had lived, taking an aperitif where Hemingway had once sat drinking, watching an organ-grinder in a square in Montmartre. And again they ended the day at the Deux Magots, sipping cognac with ice.

Sometimes Craig took Fay's arm as they went down to the Métro. Once he gently and efficiently removed a speck of dust from her eye. His closeness then was a torment and a defeat because it seemed patently obvious that her nearness aroused no response in him.

This time she didn't invite rejection by suggesting that he had a meal at her apartment, and he didn't seem to expect it. He merely picked up the portfolio and thanked her for a lovely day. 'See you some time,' he said, and she heard his quick footsteps as he ran down the stairs. Almost as if he couldn't wait to get away, she thought miserably.

But two days later a vast sheaf of spring flowers arrived. There was no note, but instinctively Fay knew that they were from Craig. What a strange, unpredictable, quixotic man, she thought happily, hunting out all her vases and pots. She wondered when he would come again. Did the flowers mean that things had changed? Were they a—a message, or simply a way of thanking her for a few pleasant hours? The last thing she saw before she slept was the tiny bud vase by her bed holding a single daffodil. The first thing to greet her when she came in from work each evening was the scent of freesia in the hall.

She had to recognise now that she had fallen in love. She hadn't been prepared for it to happen like this. It was such a precarious emotion—especially when the man involved was Craig. And emotions could create such havoc when one particular person became all-important. Hadn't she seen that in her own family? Until now she had managed to steer clear of it. That was why she had valued Christophe's affection; he still allowed her to be her own person. He had posed no threats. Poor Christophe. She bit her lip, thinking with a pang of his predictability and his utter decency. If she hadn't met Craig she would still be deluding herself that those virtues were all she wanted.

What a fool I was, she thought, touching a blue iris with a gentle forefinger. I thought I had things all neatly worked out. I thought I was in control.

* * *

When Claudia arrived a fortnight later she found Fay hanging new curtains after an energetic spate of painting. The room sparkled. New lampshades cast soft apricot shadows over the cream linen sofa and the shaggy off-white rug.

'Goodness,' Claudia exclaimed gaily, 'I seem to have come at a bad time! You *do* look busy.'

Hastily Fay pulled off the bandanna she had wound around her head. 'Come in, Claudia. Just catching up on things,' she explained lamely, fighting down the disappointment of seeing her stepmother instead of Craig.

Claudia was watching her with veiled amusement, as if sensing that her visit was not altogether welcome. 'Such a pleasant room,' she murmured, glancing around. 'Oh, I know I've seen it before, but somehow you always seem to introduce fresh, individual touches. That lamp... I haven't seen *it* before...' Then she went to the window. 'Not that I personally would care to live off the Boul. Mich.' She laughed.

'But I like it here. Dry Martini?' Deftly Fay mixed the drink in response to Claudia's nod. Trust Claudia to arrive looking as if she had just stepped out of a beauty salon at the very moment when Fay looked shiny and dishevelled. Strange that it wouldn't have mattered with Craig, she thought wonderingly, in spite of his sophistication. Hastily she switched her thoughts back, trying to give all her attention to Claudia's chatter about her own home in Cannes.

'Of course, it's frightfully expensive,' Claudia went on reflectively, 'but I eke out a modest living by taking small jobs.' As Fay raised her eyebrows she went on, 'Nothing too arduous, of course, but... Well, I do a little caretaking sometimes for friends who're going away for any length of time. That allows me to let my own apartment for those weeks, so it's quite lucrative. Oh, I look after the occasional pet, or meet people's relatives at the airport and ferry them around. Quite a varied schedule, I suppose you would say.' She smiled and sipped her drink. 'Sometimes I receive payment in kind, small gifts, you know. It makes me feel less of a serf.'

Fay watched her guardedly, recognising that if Vicky's suspicions were right this could be the opening gambit before Claudia really got down to business. Fay wondered distractedly if Claudia was hoping to stay for a few days, and her spirit shrank. But Claudia kept the conversation light, sitting like a polite, amusing acquaintance in spite of the bitter shared memories. 'And of course,' she resumed, 'I can always sell the gifts, and that helps a little.'

She paused, watching Fay over her glass. 'But now that Julius is dead I can't pretend that things are going to be easy for me. I often wish that I'd had the benefit of some specialised training. Like you. You're very lucky, you know, Fay.'

Fay returned her gaze steadily. 'It wasn't only luck, Claudia. Hard work and resolution *did* play a part.' And, she added silently, if you had had your way I would have ended up as a—as a clerk, haphazardly picking up my job as I went along. It was only through Father's support that I was ever allowed to go to the art college.

'Oh, well, of course.' Claudia's ripple of laughter held a note of patronage. 'I wasn't implying——' Then she sighed. 'Oh, if only your father had patched up that silly old quarrel with Julius...' She stared down at her glass with gentle sorrow. 'And so you, my dear, have inherited Brantye. You don't mean to tell me now that you're not lucky! It has got to be worth quite a lot of money.'

'Yes, I suppose so. I haven't really thought much about it,' Fay murmured. Craig had possessed her thoughts, one way or another, and for some reason she had held back from the final, irrevocable act of having the house put on the market.

Claudia looked up, her eyes wide. 'Do you really mean to tell me that you haven't already weighed up the probable financial benefits of inheriting a place like that?' she said slowly. 'Heavens above, you must be even luckier than I had thought! Now if Brantye were mine I would have had it valued straight away, and it would be up for sale at this very moment. You *will* be selling it, of course?'

'Yes, I expect I will.'

'Of *course* you will.' Claudia laughed. 'I must say I'm amazed that such a sensible, competent person as yourself hasn't put all that in hand before now.' She paused for a moment, then went on silkily, 'You know, Fay, your father wasn't exactly wealthy. And bringing up you and Vicky wasn't exactly a picnic.'

Nor for us, Fay wanted to retort, but she said slowly, 'No, I suppose not. You were young to have two adolescents thrust upon you and——'

'Yes. And adolescents don't come cheaply.'

Fay had an overwhelming desire to snap, Get on with it, Claudia. Come to the point. Instead she said quietly, 'I was under the impression that Grandfather helped.'

'Oh, well, a little, of course,' Claudia murmured. 'But I was never cut out to carry a begging bowl. However, in the circumstances... Oh, I know that we're not exactly flesh and blood, but you and Vicky are the only family I have. And families should stick together.' She widened her eyes candidly. 'That's one reason why I tried to patch up the quarrel between your father and Julius.'

Lies! Fay thought wretchedly. For two pins she would have made an excuse about having to go out, and hurried Claudia away. Her stepmother's knack of twisting words or situations to her own advantage had never been more evident. If I didn't know you, Fay thought, I might be taken in by all this. But I *do* know you. And besides, Vicky warned me of the line you might take.

Claudia hesitated, as if to gave Fay the opportunity to speak, but when Fay remained silent she went on a little more sharply, 'If I'm forced to spell it out, my dear, then... Well, if you felt like—shall we say *sharing*?—a little of your good fortune, especially as it doesn't seem to mean a great deal to you in financial terms, then you wouldn't find me—unappreciative. I have a friend who does well with investments. But to invest, one needs capital. And that's all I lack, just a little capital to yield a small income.'

She smiled, and Fay was struck afresh by her loveliness. The years hadn't dimmed her looks, rather they had matured a beauty that would probably be there until the day Claudia died. And her flair for choosing the right clothes, hairstyle and make-up had created a woman who would always turn men's heads. 'You see,' Claudia went on appealingly, 'I *did* give up some of my best years...'

It was blackmail, Fay thought, trying to harden her heart as Claudia's movement to put down her glass brought into play the sparkle of the diamond she wore on a fine platinum chain at her throat. From the blue shoes to the blue and white spotted linen suit, and beautifully cut and tinted hair, she seemed to ooze affluence and ease.

'Actually,' Fay prevaricated, 'I'm not quite sure what I'm doing about Brantye. Nothing's absolutely definite yet, Claudia.' Why don't I just tell her to go? she thought miserably. Why don't I expose her for the hypocrite she really is? And yet, once, long ago, Claudia had made her father happy, had snapped him out of the agonies of bereavement. Fay might not like her stepmother, but perhaps she did owe her something. 'I need to think about Brantye,' she concluded lamely.

Claudia was too clever to reveal her disappointment. 'Of course,' she murmured. 'Please don't think I'm trying to rush things.' She glanced at her watch. 'I must go. I have a dinner date. I'm going back to England tomorrow to join some friends in Cumbria. I thought I might stop off and see Vicky in her play. I'll phone you some time. We could lunch together the next time I'm here.'

'Yes, do,' Fay murmured automatically, relieved that the interview was over even though nothing had been resolved. But surely there must be more worthwhile things to do with the proceeds of Brantye than merely cushion Claudia's extravagances!

She followed Claudia out into the hall. An arrangement of the remainder of Craig's flowers stood on the oak chest. Claudia fingered one with a gloved hand. 'You always loved flowers,' she mused. 'Even on that last day with your father you were——' She stopped as Fay's expression froze. 'But these are lovely,' she went on smoothly. 'French boyfriends can be so thoughtful.'

'As a matter of fact, they're the survivors of a huge bouquet which Craig sent me,' Fay said coolly, still angered by Claudia's pointed reminder of her own part in her father's death.

'Really?' For a moment Claudia's eyes narrowed, then she laughed, recovering herself. 'Craig can be so attentive, can't he?' she murmured. 'He always observes the little niceties. A huge bouquet, you say? Rather extravagant of him, though, considering the heavy sums he dissipates on his various conservation whims . . .' Her expression sharpened suddenly. 'Have you seen him recently?'

Fay nodded. 'He's been over to Paris a few times.'

'How nice for you. Strange that he never mentioned it,' Claudia said quietly.

'Oh?' Fay's heart paused for a second. '*You've* seen him, then? Lately?'

'Only last weekend. We went up to Scotland. I wanted to see Margaret Farrand—an old friend—and as Craig had business in the area we drove up together.'

A sudden pain ripped through Fay as she visualised Claudia, her elegant legs outstretched in the long silver-grey car. They must have stopped for meals somewhere en route—maybe even spent a night at a hotel... So for several hours Claudia would have had Craig's undivided attention. What might she have achieved in that time? By Craig's own admission, he was a man and Claudia an attractive woman...

With difficulty Fay brought her thoughts under control. 'How nice,' she said offhandedly, 'that you were company for each other.'

'That's what *I* thought. The Farrands have a gorgeous place, and there was quite a house party. When I explained that Craig had driven me up they naturally asked him to stay. And, of course, they were *charmed* by him.' Claudia paused, a reminiscent smile on her lovely mouth. 'We had a wonderful time. There's something about him, I find... The confidence of a man at ease *anywhere*, that masculine grace which some men have and others will *never* have... Not to mention that exciting suggestion of—power.'

'Ye-es,' Fay murmured, wishing that Claudia hadn't chosen to voice her own private feelings about Craig.

'You don't sound too sure,' Claudia observed. 'But believe me, my dear, Craig has power, all right. Don't underestimate him. What he wants, he gets. In *all* spheres.'

'I don't think I understand,' Fay began faintly. 'You make him sound utterly ruthless.'

'Well, he is,' Claudia said emphatically. 'You have only to take his obsession with conservation, for example. He managed—and it could only have been through unremitting pressure on the powers-that-be—to get a road-widening scheme diverted simply to retain some tiny village lock-up that's existed for centuries. And Fairlie Wood.... Again, it's thanks to his intervention that the place was preserved and not sold for building land. He sank a great deal of money into that particular project, wining and dining the right people, mounting a publicity campaign and so forth. If he had been born in a different age, he would have been a most effective rabble-rouser.' She laughed. 'That type of man can be lethal to the female heart.' She gave Fay's arm a light tap. 'So do be careful, Fay. Watch your step with him. We both know he's devastatingly attractive, and I should hate to see *you* get hurt,' she finished complacently.

Fay managed to match Claudia's laugh, although in her own ears it sounded hollow and forced. 'Really, Claudia! I'm not so stupid as to exaggerate the importance of my place in Craig's life. And I certainly have no intention of getting hurt!'

'Intentions have nothing to do with it,' Claudia said wisely. 'And if he's taken to popping over to Paris... Still,' she shrugged, 'I'm sure you don't need any advice from me. You've always managed your affairs very well, I'm sure. But in the event of heartbreak—and I know you wouldn't be the first to suffer from Craig's passing interest—don't say I didn't warn you!'

Fay's smile felt as if it had been starched painfully across her face. 'Don't worry about me, Claudia. Thanks for the warning, but I can assure you it isn't necessary. As you have so often said, I'm perfectly capable of looking after myself.'

CHAPTER SEVEN

RESOLUTELY Fay tried to put Claudia's visit out of her mind. But some underlying suggestion in her stepmother's words and expressions lingered disturbingly.

In Honfleur Craig had succeeded in convincing Fay that Claudia was no more than a friend. But now...? Claudia was so attractive and would pull out all the stops to get what she wanted.

Angry at the demoralising effect that Claudia's visit had on her, Fay thought of the hours she and Craig had spent together. But if he was the charmer that Claudia had suggested, there was no way of knowing that those hours meant as much to him as they did to Fay. As for the flowers... According to Claudia they were just a courtesy. Perhaps, in truth, they meant nothing more than just that.

With unnecessary vigour Fay washed and dried the glasses, firmly closing the cupboard door. Back in the living-room she found some background music on the radio and tried to give her mind to developing her earlier idea of a range of knitwear based on the subdued colours of the old furnishings of Brantye.

On Wednesday Giselle mentioned a film that she would like to see, and Fay suggested they went together.

'Where's Christophe?' Giselle looked up from the pile of magazines she was leafing through. 'You haven't said much about him lately.'

'He was ill. I told you.' Fay sat back, lacing her fingers behind her head. 'Right now he's in Menton with a wealthy client. His mother is joining him and they're going on a cruise. Her health, you know.' Fay grinned. 'Apparently Christophe's indisposition took its toll of her.'

Giselle grimaced. 'You'll have to watch her,' she murmured. 'Possessive mothers can be demons.'

'The thought had struck me,' Fay answered noncommittally, picking up her pen again.

She was rather relieved that Christophe was away; it shelved at least one problem for a little while. Privately Fay wondered if Madame Lefèvre had played a part in the break-up of Christophe's marriage. Had his sense of tradition and family duty finally driven his wife away? Fay didn't know the facts behind the divorce, but it was possible, she supposed. And was Madame Lefèvre's poor health an excuse to keep Christophe away from Fay for a while? That, too, seemed believable. Although if that was the case, then unwittingly she had done Fay a favour, giving her a breathing space.

On the following Friday evening Craig telephoned. 'I'm coming over tomorrow,' he told her, 'just to check what you did this time with the flowers I sent.'

His deep voice held a teasing note, and Fay answered him gaily. 'I turned the apartment into a bower, that's what I did. But most of them are gone now.'

'Is that a hint?' he said. 'If so, I've taken it.'

'Good.' She laughed. 'I knew that I wouldn't have to spell it out.' Her heart had leapt at the sound of his voice. She felt incredibly elated and wondered if it showed in her voice. Steady! she told herself sternly, remembering Claudia's warning. 'I suppose it's business again?' she asked lightly.

'No. Strictly pleasure. So I'm warning you or, rather, giving you advance notice. Also I've got one or two things which were left in the house. Some of your father's papers—old school reports and so forth. I thought you would like to have them.'

'I would,' Fay said. 'Thank you.'

'Until tomorrow, then. I should be with you by, say, seven.' He rang off abruptly.

The following evening Fay was in the shower when the doorbell rang. Shrugging into her housecoat, and clutching it around her, she let him in, her eyes shining, her tawny hair tumbling in disarray about her flushed face.

'I'm a little early,' he remarked evenly, as he followed her into the room. 'I'm taking you out to dinner. I've booked a table at a small place in Montmartre.' He looked at his watch. 'You have exactly forty minutes.'

'You're being very dictatorial,' she remarked meekly.

'Yes, very,' he agreed. 'Oh, these are the papers I mentioned.'

Fay glanced down. In the transparent plastic folder she recognised a birthday card which she had designed and sent to her father years ago. For a moment her expression dimmed.

'Thank you,' she murmured, leaning sideways to drop the package on the coffee-table. The movement caused her yellow housecoat to slip a little from one shoulder, revealing the gentle sweep of her upper breast. She straightened quickly, pulling the neckline closer and moving away, slightly embarrassed. But Craig had noticed. His face was suddenly, frighteningly intent, the bland imperturbability gone.

'Come here,' he said, not moving his lips, his eyes holding her own gaze compellingly. Roughly he cupped her face in his hands, raising it so that his lips covered her own. Then his arms were around her, crushing her violently to him. 'You witch,' he whispered thickly against her mouth. 'How do you expect a man *not* to be bewitched?'

His hands began to move over the satin, smoothing her hips, her waist, up, up sensuously over her back and her shoulders, then curving to cup her breasts. Inside Fay a thrill broke, a tiny, delicate ripple, gathering force and momentum with each movement of his hands, until it broke in a crescendo and she gasped. His mouth claimed hers again with deliberate mastery, his tongue flicking her own, playing savagely with all her responses as if moulding them into the answer he demanded. And she could only cling to him, her body throbbing with a desire that weakened her.

At last he put her from him abruptly. 'Stand up, girl.' His tone was grim. 'Go and get dressed. We now have——' he glanced at his watch '—exactly thirty-two minutes.' He turned away.

For a moment she stared at him wonderingly, baffled by the apparent ease with which he could switch off his emotions. Then, without a word, and unable to think straight, she went into the bedroom, her own emotions churning inside her.

When she came out she had changed into a pearl-grey dress. Her cool appearance belied the dizzy uncertainty of her feelings. He stood up immediately she came into the room, his gaze lingering over the grey suede shoes, the grey gossamer sheen of her legs, and the swathe of thin suede that whittled her waist and matched the colour of her garnet earrings. Something in his stare brought the bright colour leaping back into her face, and she said faintly, 'Well, will I do?'

'Need you ask? Do you want me to pay you compliments?'

'Only if you want to,' she whispered.

'We'll go into all that later.' He took her jacket from her and draped it over her shoulders.

He had reserved a table at a tiny, intimate restaurant up on the heights of Montmartre. The May evening was warm, but here above the lights of Paris a tiny breeze cooled the warmth of Fay's skin. She felt that Craig had lit a flame in her, and she was thankful for the terrace table.

During the meal they talked, after a few stilted remarks resuming the ease of other hours spent together in Paris, identifying the various floodlit buildings and the strewn lights that made the city at night seem like a magic, earth-bound constellation.

Craig didn't mention his trip to Scotland, and Fay didn't intend asking about it. These moments were too precious to allow the interjection of anything reminiscent of Claudia.

'It's so beautiful up here,' Fay said at last with a sigh, as coffee and cognac were brought to them.

Craig nodded. 'I think I can understand your thralldom,' he said drily. 'No second thoughts about Brantye, I suppose? I notice that it hasn't been put up for sale yet.'

Fay shook her head, her earrings glowing in the lamp-light. 'I'm sticking to my decision about it,' she murmured, twisting the stem of her brandy glass, 'but I'm finding it rather hard to act upon. Old strings, I suppose... Roots pulling...' Then she laughed, lifting her head. 'It's all totally illogical, of course. One morning I shall wake up, telephone Mr Seymour, tell him to set the wheels in motion, and that will be it.'

Craig nodded thoughtfully and gestured for the bill, swallowed the last of his cognac, and helped Fay into her jacket. For a moment she wished that he hadn't raised the subject of the old house. She still had this utterly irrational feeling of loyalty to it—and, through it, to her own family. All quite ludicrous, she reminded herself. Her life was the present and the future, not the past which, heaven knew, had held more than its share of problems.

Craig had reserved a room for himself at a hotel on the rue Balzac, and, although it was quite late when they left the restaurant, Fay experienced a keen sense of loss that they had come to the end of the evening.

But this time Craig didn't hurry away. Once inside her apartment he came to stand behind her, taking her coat from her shoulders, lifting the mass of hair to drop tiny shivering kisses on her neck. Her breath caught and he turned her to face him, drawing her closer and looking down at her for a long moment. 'I want you,' he said harshly. 'You know that, don't you?' He accompanied his words with a tiny shake. 'But more than that. I want you—as my *wife*.' There was a relentless lack of tenderness, almost an anger, in his voice that Fay couldn't understand. His words had exploded in her brain in a firestorm of joy, but his tone disturbed and alarmed her.

'I—I don't understand,' she faltered. 'When we've been together—recently—you——'

'Didn't touch you? Is that what you're saying?' He gave a wintry smile. 'I had my reasons. My recollection of the time when I did—touch you—that evening in Vicky's flat—was only too painful. By heaven, I thought, the next time I kiss her she's going to *welcome* me. Of course, I slipped a little that night in your hall——'

'And then you rushed away. You'd remembered something,' Fay said faintly.

'It was too soon. I wanted you then. I've always wanted you . . . But,' he gave a slightly grim smile, 'shall we say that sometimes discretion is the better part of valour?'

Fay stared up at him, noting the rock-hard jaw, the narrowed, sombre eyes. Then she took a deep breath. 'Did you really mean it—that you wanted to marry me?'

'Oh, yes,' he clipped out. 'That's what I want.'

Fay swallowed. Her heart was doing crazy things to her blood. He wanted marriage. But in some baffling way, this didn't seem like a proposal, merely a statement of fact. And a fact which didn't appear to give him much pleasure. She didn't know what to say. It might have been laughable—except that it wasn't. One thing was sure, Craig Mackenzie was a hellishly difficult man to understand. 'I'll get the coffee,' she whispered lamely at last.

'Later.' His eyes still held her gaze, and she found herself unable to look away. She could only stare at the darkness of hair and eyes, the carved cleft of his chin, the resolution written in his face. She wanted to tell him that marrying him was the only thing she wanted. Yet something held her back. She shivered, excited, afraid, unsure.

Then he bent his head and kissed her. His mouth was disconcertingly patient and tender, his lips merely touching hers glancingly, letting go, brushing her mouth like gentle wing-beats, shaping it into quick, tentative movements as if to answer his own strange mood. There was a silken warmth in his lips that Fay found almost unbearably sensuous and frustratingly tantalising.

He unbuttoned the front of her dress so slowly that she barely felt the movement of his hands until his fingers touched her bare skin, and a quiver ran through her as she heard the sudden hiss of her breath. Sensations rippled through her like pulse-beats, driving her blood. Softly, but with resolute intent, he cupped her breasts, his thumbs brushing her nipples as delicately as a breath until they stiffened with desire, all reason lost to her now. 'You like it,' he whispered. 'Don't you? *Don't* you?'

She could only shake her head wordlessly, not caring what answer she gave. She only wanted this moment to last forever, to go on and on, flying her to greater heights, as an elemental force stronger than will-power held her there against him.

His head moved down and his tongue continued the teasing until Fay realised that the broken moan she heard came from her own mouth, buried in his hair.

'I don't have to tell you again that I want you,' he said roughly. 'And if there's any honesty in that prim, prudent heart of yours, you'll admit that you want me. Tonight's the time for honesty. Starting with *now*.' His mouth swooped down hungrily to meet her own. One hand slid behind her shoulders, the other moved down to the back of her thighs as he lifted her, and she could feel his strong, steady heartbeat against her shoulder.

Her bedroom door was open, and the gleam of her triple mirror shone with a mysterious, ghostly light. Bemused, she watched as it was filled by their reflections, then it blanked again, and she was lying on her bed.

Slowly he began to undress her, his fingers lingering and unhurried. She seemed unable to move, lost in a swirl of responsive desire. When his hands finally moved down her legs, smoothing off the grey silk stockings, she began to tremble uncontrollably.

Quickly he undressed, and when he came to her and she felt the touch of his flesh she turned to him in a wild, strong surrender that cleansed her of all inhibitions.

She revelled in the scent of his body, the feel of his strong limbs caressing and entwining with her own. She gave herself joyfully to a million sensations of arousal as he found the tender secret roots of sexual pleasure.

And, as if of their own volition, and in answer to some dark, atavistic knowledge, her hands explored the smooth skin of broad shoulders, the roughness of his chest, the lean economy of his hips... Craig groaned suddenly then moved, his hands under her hips, lifting her to receive him in a rhythm as old and deep as time.

Inside her, heat grew, swelling and spreading to suffuse her body, bearing her to a sudden, amazing triumph as Craig cried out her name hoarsely, the sound diminishing into the distance. And for a while there was nothing...

Afterwards he kissed away the tears she didn't know she had shed.

'Is it——?' she whispered, after a while.

'Is it—what?' His voice held all the darkness of this wonderful night.

'Always so—so—good?'

He raised himself on one elbow and looked down at her. 'Didn't you—know...?'

Fay couldn't see his expression, just the hard outline of his features now softened by the gloom. She shook her head. 'No. It's never happened before. Couldn't you tell?'

'I—wondered,' he said softly. He put his arms around her, pulling her close to him. 'No regrets?'

She shook her head and felt his mouth move in a smile against her bare shoulder. She began to stroke his hair tentatively, filled with a shy amazement that two bodies could solve, by a physical act, so many mental and emotional problems. 'I feel as if I've thrown off all my clothes,' she said luxuriously.

'Correction,' he whispered. '*I* threw off all your clothes.'

She laughed softly. 'So you did.' She began to nibble the lobe of his ear gently. 'But you evaded my question. Is it always so good?'

'If you keep doing that I shall be forced to demonstrate the answer—physically,' he murmured.

'But you're *still* not answering.' She felt a flicker of apprehension. His hesitation seemed to suggest that his reply must be carefully arranged.

Then he said, in a voice which she didn't recognise as his, 'It has *never* been so good.'

'And have—have there been many—women in your life?' she asked hesitantly.

She saw him smile in the darkness. 'Probably not so many as you apparently suspect.' He lay back, his hands behind his head.

How could they bear to let him go? Fay wondered sleepily...

She woke again, just after one o'clock. He was looking down at her with an unreadable expression.

'I seem to remember you came here for coffee,' she began drowsily.

'That was a long time ago,' he murmured.

'I know.' In another age.

'All the same, I'd better leave.' He drew back the cover, and Fay marvelled that she felt no embarrassment as he looked down at her body, pale in the darkness. 'Adorable,' he murmured. Then abruptly he turned away.

An unbearable stab of pain ran through Fay. He was leaving her, going... But why? He could have stayed here for the weekend. She had more or less taken it for granted that he would. Useless, a little inner voice reminded her, to take anything for granted where Craig was concerned. '*Must* you go?' she said lightly, her casual tone masking her sense of loss.

'I'm afraid so. Didn't I tell you that I'm heavily involved in a seminar this weekend with the conservation people? Well, perhaps I had too many more pressing matters on my mind.' He smiled briefly as he knotted his tie.

Fay got out of bed, shrugging into the heavy satin housecoat. 'I'll make you some coffee,' she said, and went into the kitchen. Automatically her hands obeyed the routine of years. How strange, she thought, that they, too, were part of this body that knew a spent and languorous ache, a faint, delicious hurt. And now he was going back to Sussex, back to a life in which she had no part.

He drank his coffee in silence, his face composed and rather remote. It puzzled her to see his self-control when she felt so weak and vulnerable.

He set down his cup, then he drew her to her feet. He put up a hand, and with one finger traced her profile down from the hair growing in a widow's peak, over her forehead, nose, lips and chin, along the line of her throat down to the shadow between her breasts. He bent and laid his mouth there for a moment.

'Don't forget me, Fay,' he said very softly. 'But just in case you do, I'll be back.'

'Soon?' she asked weakly.

He nodded. 'Very soon.' Then he added, 'And—Christophe?'

Fay smiled, understanding immediately. 'He's away,' she murmured, 'but I'll tell him. Just as soon as he gets back.'

'You do that,' Craig said, whispering against her lips. 'I don't intend to share you with anyone.'

* * *

Craig came over to Paris on the two Fridays following. On these occasions he didn't reserve a hotel room for himself, but stayed at Fay's apartment until late on the Sunday afternoon.

Those weekends were like celebrations, a high peak of love. Together they saw Paris, dining by candle-light on a boat cruise along the Seine to the accompaniment of French music, and marvelling with the other tourists at the beauty of the floodlit buildings. They drank beer in small bistros near the Flea Market and usually finished off the evening at the Deux Magots.

Sometimes they would cook a meal together in Fay's apartment, pausing to sip wine, to touch and kiss each other. It was a surprise to Fay that Craig was quite an accomplished chef, although she never seemed to do justice to his cooking because of the fizz of excited longing inside. And there were the nights—nights which Fay wished would never end.

And then, after Craig had left, the flowers would come, reminders of their hours together. As if she needed reminding!

There was, however, one tiny flaw in Fay's happiness. Craig had never referred to marriage again. Each weekend she half expected him to raise the subject so that they could start making plans, setting a date. By now, she thought ruefully, Christophe would have had everything organised down to the last minor detail! But apparently that wasn't Craig's way. And it was undeniable that part of his attraction was his unpredictability. It lent a kind of magic to all they did. It wasn't beyond the bounds of credibility that he would surprise her, sweeping her suddenly into a whirlwind wedding. And always, when they were together, there was so much to talk about, so much to do.

Only after he had gone did Fay experience a little prick of anxiety that he didn't seem to be in any particular hurry. That might be for a number of reasons, she argued silently, but it was a subject which, for some reason—perhaps a lingering lack of confidence—she couldn't bring herself to raise.

Then came three weeks when Craig was busy. He told her that he had a great deal of pressing business that couldn't wait and would keep him on the move. 'I'm also scheduled for a brief lecture tour,' he added. 'You're not the only one who suffers from pressure of work.' He kissed her lingeringly. 'It's unfortunate that finance has to be a consideration of living.'

She moved sensuously in his arms. 'You're beginning to sound like Christophe,' she said with a smile.

He laughed softly in the darkness. 'Heaven forbid! Is he back yet?'

'No.' Fay's happiness dimmed fractionally. She wasn't looking forward to her next meeting with Christophe.

'Let's not waste our time together talking of him,' Craig murmured against her ear. 'Three weeks without you is going to seem like an age.'

'For me, too,' Fay said.

There was an added passion in their lovemaking that night, a kind of desperation that each second together must be filled with the touch and sound of each other. It left no room for talk about the practical aspects of a wedding.

The afterglow of lovemaking lingered, warming the next few days as Fay wondered how she would survive three weeks without Craig. Then she laughed at her own foolishness; what better reason was there for survival? Craig telephoned, once from Dublin, twice from Amsterdam. But for some reason their conversations seemed brief and unsatisfactory, almost as if distance was raising a barrier between them. And, in spite of herself, gradually tiny misgivings that must have lain in secret cells of Fay's mind began to make themselves heard. Craig had spoken of marriage, yet somehow he still seemed to remain uncommitted.

And Fay's confidence wasn't helped by a conversation with Giselle over lunch one day. Fay knew that Giselle sometimes spent weekends with her boyfriend, yet Giselle admitted that she did not love him. 'We—excite each other,' she said, her eyes shining. 'We make time—very special. It is like champagne, and I love champagne. But if I loved Arnaud—*pouf*! That is so serious. I would be buying duvets not dresses, saving money... He would have the power to make me miserable. No. I am happy with my champagne lover. I do not try to make him my 'usband.'

It was one way of looking at things, Fay conceded silently. Very practical, and very French. But it was not *her* way. Yet might it not be how Craig saw her? As a champagne girl? The thought niggled at the edges of her mind, bugging her at odd intervals during the afternoon, demanding analysis. After all, Craig had never actually spoken of *love*. He simply admitted that he had wanted her from the beginning. And that could mean something entirely different, as Giselle had demonstrated.

And even when he had mentioned marriage, the words had seemed wrung from him, almost against his will. So could they simply have been a device to get her into bed? Claudia's warning came back in a cold echo. He was ruthless, she had said. And, 'What he wants, he gets.'

Fay stared bleakly out of the window, wishing that her brain would stop racing. But how well did she know the man she loved? She recalled the journey to Scotland he had made with Claudia which he never mentioned, and Fay had too much pride to ask about it. So what else was hidden behind those dark, secret eyes?

Resolutely she slammed a door on such thoughts. You're getting neurotic, she scolded. As soon as you see him again, everything will be all right. Or would it? Was love already slipping away on the heels of uncertainty? The trouble with you, my girl, she told herself severely, is that you've seen in your own family how fickle love can be. And now it's happened to you you're not prepared to trust it.

Now, more than ever, those three weeks began to seem like three years.

Then Christophe returned, and, with a sinking heart at the prospect ahead, Fay agreed to meet him for dinner.

He looked tanned and fit. He had met several interesting and useful people on the cruise, he said, and his mother had benefited enormously from the holiday. Had he always seemed so smug? Fay wondered. Or was it the contrast with Craig that made him suddenly middle-aged and sleekly self-satisfied?

Side by side, sipping *apéritifs* on the red banquette in the *salon* of a hotel, Fay felt his arm slide into hers as he said softly, 'What have you been doing, *chérie*?'

She gave a nervous smile. 'Oh, working madly, of coursc, and...' She swallowed. 'Christophe, there's——' The arrival of large menus cut her short.

After they had ordered she tried to summon up courage again to tell him that she wouldn't be seeing him any more, but before she could speak, he said, 'You are invited to dinner at home tomorrow night.'

Fay looked down, fumbling in her handbag. 'I'm—sorry...' Her voice was muted, and Christophe bent closer to catch her words. She looked up then, squaring her shoulders and meeting his gaze frankly. 'Christophe, I'm sorry. I can't come.'

'Oh?' His blue eyes looked hurt. 'I was hoping to make the evening very special. I intended to announce——'

'No!' The word came so sharply that two people at the next table stared. Fay moistened her lips. 'I—I think I know what you're going to say. But please don't say it.' She gazed up at him, her eyes wide and appealing, begging for his perception.

He stared at her in silence for a moment, and somehow she found the courage to go on. 'Christophe, I think a great deal of you. But not enough. I thought I did. I can't keep on saying I'm sorry, but I *am* sorry. Please believe that.' Dismayed, she felt tears sting her eyes and surreptitiously she brushed them away with her forefinger. She had said it all, yet it sounded abrupt and cruel.

His mouth tightened, but at that moment they were called to their table. Miserably Fay picked at her lobster. But Christophe quickly recovered himself, chatting inconsequentially about the ports where his ship had called. He nodded greetings across the room to people whom he knew. Fay had to admire his poise, yet somehow it only emphasised the awful pathos of the occasion.

Over coffee he said carefully, in a low voice, 'Obviously I had hoped for a warmer welcome home. You've been different ever since you came back from England. You're worried about selling that family house of yours, and you've been working too hard. Perhaps you are feeling—how do you say it?—pressurised?'

Dismally Fay shook her head. 'It's not that. It's just that—something's happened, and I know now that——'

But he held up a brown, well-manicured hand. 'Do not say any more tonight. We've known each other a long time. Do not end it in a few minutes. I could give you a good life. You will no longer work, no longer be pressurised.'

'Christophe—please! I'm trying to——'

'I will not listen. These things must be thought over carefully. I think you should take a holiday. After that, we can talk again.'

'Is that the way you do business?' Fay stifled a hysterical desire to laugh. She had known that this would be difficult and painful, but hadn't dreamed that Christophe would adopt such a sensible, obstructionist attitude.

He frowned. 'Big decisions demand a great deal of consideration,' he reproved. 'As I've said, we'll talk about it again when you're more relaxed. You may feel differently then.'

Fay stared into her brandy glass. Time wouldn't make any difference to her decision, but perhaps tonight would blunt the final edge for Christophe. The alternative was to protest more vehemently, but that might mean a small scene in public, and Christophe would hate that.

'I won't feel—differently,' she persisted in a tiny voice.

'How can you know?' He called for the bill.

In the car, Fay said, 'You asked me how I could know that I won't feel differently. But I do know. You see, I've—met someone else. It may not even work out. But it's shown me that I can't go back to being the person I thought I was.'

He was silent until they reached her apartment, then he said, 'Now I understand. An Englishman?' When Fay nodded, he went on. 'Then you were right. There is no more to be said.'

Fay leaned over to kiss his cheek with cold lips. 'Please don't be too hurt. It couldn't have worked for us. I see that now. There would have been something missing—

for both of us. Take care, Christophe, dear. And good—goodbye.'

Fiercely she blinked back her tears as she went upstairs. There, it was over, but relief wouldn't come just yet.

As she reached her front door she heard the telephone ringing. But by the time she had found her key it had stopped. Damn. It could have been Craig. She needed him. Just the sound of his voice would help so much.

She stared at the silent phone for a little while without seeing it. Where was Craig? Back in England—yes, he would be starting on the lecture tour tomorrow. So possibly he was at home. He wouldn't be in bed yet, for English time was one hour behind French time. She dialled quickly, listened to the ringing tone for a few moments, heard it stop as the receiver was taken off. Her heart began to bump loudly.

Then Claudia's voice answered.

Silently Fay replaced the receiver and sank down on her knees, her forehead pressed against the smooth wooden edge of the low table.

CHAPTER EIGHT

WITH dry, burning eyes Fay stared at her bedside clock. Sleep was as far away as ever. One way and another, this evening had assumed the qualities of a nightmare.

Claudia at Craig's house. Was he there, too? There could be several reasons why he hadn't answered the telephone. And if he was there, what were they doing? Fay's mind shuddered away from any possible answers. Had he been playing a double game all along?

She closed her eyes, willing sleep to come. She needed oblivion, but her brain was wide awake. In her mind's eye she saw The Lodge where he lived, and then, beyond it, the dark bulk of Brantye. Brantye... Where it had all begun. Fay tossed restlessly. She had still done nothing about selling the house, merely writing to Mr Seymour telling him that she would let him have her instructions in due course. She didn't even know whether or not Craig had removed his furniture. As if by mutual tacit consent, neither she nor Craig had spoken of Brantye since that evening at the restaurant high up in Montmartre. Just as, in the same way, Claudia's name had never cropped up in their conversations since their trip to Honfleur. Both Brantye and Claudia were prickly obstacles which would have marred the perfection of the recent wonderful weekends.

The days dragged, filled with a dull, pervasive ache. She worked late every night, going home to fall into a thick, unrefreshing sleep. There were no more flowers. Perhaps Craig would never come to Paris again. Maybe their love-affair was already over, and this was his way of letting her know.

The following Tuesday a letter arrived from Vicky. Fay opened it apprehensively. Vicky rarely wrote, preferring instead to telephone occasionally or, when she wasn't working, to come over for brief visits.

Quickly Fay scanned the hasty scrawl, seeming to hear Vicky's breathless, amused voice. Until Craig's name leapt off the page.

'You'll never guess who came backstage the other night,' Vicky wrote. 'Claudia—on her way back from somewhere up north. She took me out to supper after the show. We could have done with her in the audience—we're playing to very thin houses. She was at her glamorous and sparkling best. She mentioned Craig Mackenzie a great deal and said that she had been in Cumbria with him...'

Stricken, Fay folded the letter and tucked it into its envelope. Now, it seemed, she had her answer—not that she hadn't instinctively guessed it.

The week moved along on dragging feet. Only for brief moments was Fay able to wrench her thoughts away from her own unhappiness to concentrate on other things. How stupid she had been! How utterly juvenile to react in the way she had to a man who had merely exploded into her life and shown her what she had never had eyes to see before!

The cold, sick feeling expanded in her stomach. She had only herself to blame—immersed in work, in creating an orderly kind of life and avoiding any heavy relationships, what else could she expect than, come the first dynamically charismatic man to storm into her safe little world, she made him her be-all and end-all? Pathetic! It was entirely her own fault for lowering her guard without knowing how vulnerable she really was.

'You look as if you need a holiday,' Giselle said with merciless candour on Friday. 'Why don't you slow down? Come out with us tonight. I'll get Arnaud to bring a friend. I know a very chic disco... How about it?'

'Thanks, but not tonight.' Fay smiled at her friend. 'I'll work late again. There's still this wretched spec sheet to do...' Wearily she pushed her hair back from her hot forehead.

'There you go!' Giselle exclaimed. '*Alors!* Is it that you like having the dark shadows below your eyes?'

Fay managed a laugh.

But Giselle was right, she admitted that evening, catching a brutally honest reflection of herself in the hall mirror when she got home.

With no interest in food, she forced herself to prepare a salad, and was slicing cucumber when the doorbell rang. She stiffened, her heart knocking. Friday was Craig's evening... But that seemed the remotest of possibilities in the present circumstances. And, anyway, did she really want to see him? To give that ever-present knife another twist?

Or it could be Claudia, and that would be just as bad. Fay's heart was chilled, and for a moment she considered ignoring the bell. But if it was Claudia, there was little to be gained by postponing their meeting, and the older woman would simply come back tomorrow.

Biting her lip, Fay fluffed out her hair, found the shoes which she had kicked off earlier, and went into the hall as the bell rang again with peremptory violence. Apprehensively she opened the door.

Then there was only Craig's breath in her hair, the hardness of his arms around her, the movement of his leg as he toed the door closed behind him. Fay swallowed a sob, unable to look at him. Her eyes might reveal too much.

'Something wrong?' he said warily, after a moment. 'Or have I come to the wrong apartment?'

'N-no. No, of course not,' she whispered. 'It's just that I—I wasn't expecting you...'

His eyebrows winged up incredulously. '*Really?* You *do* surprise me,' he murmured, his eyes shining with a steely glint as he watched her closely. 'I *did* say three weeks.'

'Yes, but—but you haven't phoned lately——'

'I *have* tried. Anyway, I'm not much of a bloke for telephone calls. You should know that by now. And I did tell you that I was going to be very busy, dashing hither and yon. Surely you took it for granted that I'd be here tonight?' His hands held her shoulders like iron clamps. 'Or didn't you? Don't tell me that you've made other arrangements for the weekend.' He frowned savagely. 'Christophe?'

Fay shook her head. 'That's finished,' she said, 'in accordance with your instructions.' A little blaze of anger lit her. What right had he to assume that she would always be here, all other activities suspended as she waited for him to come—especially now, in the light of what she knew about him and Claudia? 'I take *nothing* for granted,' she said bitingly. 'At least nothing that involves another person.' Especially *you*, a silent voice added in her head. Her earlier life had taught her the folly of putting too much trust in a person, and the past miserable days had driven home the lesson again. 'But, since you ask, no, I haven't made any arrangements for the weekend.'

'Good, I'm glad to hear it.' He paused, then said with an edge of impatience in his voice, 'I somehow get the feeling that I ought to go out and come back again, by which time you might be more approachable.'

'Oh, I suppose you'd better come in,' Fay murmured wearily.

'I've had more enthusiastic invitations,' he snapped, 'but if that's the best you can do I suppose I'll have to be satisfied with it.'

He dropped his bag on the sofa, and Fay went to the side table to pour drinks for them both. She was finding it hard to sustain her anger when all she wanted was to run into his arms. Yet, for her own self-preservation, she must try to distance herself from him. 'I'll get some ice,' she said, conscious that he was watching her with a probing, speculative expression, obviously looking for some clue to her baffling mood.

'I hadn't realised that you were seeing so much of Claudia,' she flung over her shoulder as she went out. She wished that she had the courage to stay and watch his face. But would it tell her anything? Had he *ever* really told her anything? All she knew was that he had wanted her, and that as a lover he hadn't been disappointed. She blinked fiercely as she ran the tap over the ice tray.

There was an almost imperceptible pause before he said blandly, 'Claudia? Oh, she comes and goes.'

His tone sounded innocent enough, but as Fay went back into the other room she noticed the tight line of his lips and the slightly dilated nostrils. 'Do you mind?' he went on.

Fay managed a laugh. 'Why should I? We're both free agents, after all.'

'*Are* we?' His voice was ominously quiet as he put down his glass with sudden force, reached out and pulled her roughly down beside him. 'What the hell's got into you tonight, Fay?' he said savagely.

'Nothing,' she protested. 'But you turn up, out of the blue, and——'

She stopped as he picked up his bag. For a moment she thought that he was going to leave. Well, she debated stoically, wasn't that better than this torment? Pinning her hopes on an over-valued relationship that had existed only in her fantasies?

But he was unzipping the bag. He took out a bottle of champagne. 'See this?' he barked. 'A high-class drink—for a high-class lady? Had the devil of a job to winkle this vintage out of a wine buff I know... I'd thought we might celebrate.'

Remembering Giselle's remark about champagne, Fay felt hysterical laughter rise in her throat and drowned it with a sip of white wine. 'And what would we be celebrating? Anything special?' she said coolly.

After a moment he said tersely, 'That would depend upon you.' His eyes were like jet as they searched her face, and Fay wondered if he could see through her unhappiness to the damped-down thrill of seeing him again. 'Come here, Fay,' he said, with dangerous softness.

Fay sat perfectly still, rigid with the effort of concealing her feelings. She couldn't—*mustn't* lower this desperate barrier of reserve she had built up.

'I—see...' he breathed. He reached out suddenly, pulling her to him. His arms were bands of steel that allowed no escape. She felt herself drowning in his nearness, in the slight masculine fragrance that was part of him. His intent dominated her utterly.

His lips found her mouth angrily, crushing its softness as if he would annihilate any remaining resistance. Then, when he felt her lips part and tremble, he let her go abruptly. 'You fool,' he ground out, his eyes narrowed and angry. 'You sweet, stupid fool! Don't you know that nothing is going to come between us? Certainly not Claudia! Nor the fact that I didn't bloody well telephone you often enough!'

That kiss had taken its toll of her, and she felt weak and unequal to him. 'All right,' she murmured after a moment. 'I'm too tired to—to quarrel with you, Craig.' She paused again. 'What did you mean about a celebration?'

'Oh, I think we'll leave all that for the moment.' Craig got up briskly. 'Go and have a good hot bath and change. We're eating out.' As the defeated tears shimmered in Fay's eyes, he bent and took her face between his hands, forcing her to look into his own. 'You'll feel better. You'll see.' He laid his lips against hers fleetingly, and she felt herself begin to melt. But he drew back. 'Don't be too long,' he said. 'I'll ring and reserve a table somewhere.' Then, as she hesitated, 'Go *on,*' he commanded, turning her around in the direction of the door.

As the bathroom filled with pearly steam, Fay lay back, her eyes closed, the fragrant foam soothing against her skin. She felt physically exhausted. Just where *did* she stand with Craig? And yet...he'd turned up tonight, hadn't he? That *had* to mean something.

Fay sighed. If Craig really was the type of man that Claudia had suggested—and recent events seemed to bear that out, then... I'm a fool for loving him, Fay decided. But even *I* know that love doesn't come with a written guarantee. It's simply there—for living. But I had thought it would be a happy thing.

She didn't hear the door open, and she glanced up, startled, to see Craig standing over her. 'You *are* taking a long time,' he said sternly. Then he dropped to his knees by the bath and took the sponge from her. He began to pass it slowly over her shoulders in gentle sweeps, and she shivered voluptuously. He moved to the nape of her neck, lifting the heavy hair now curling riotously in the steam, soaping her back with the soft, scented lather. Gradually Fay began to feel all the strain and tension of the past weeks seep away, smoothed by the effortless passage of his hands over her skin.

'I've never been bathed by a man before,' she said shyly, her voice catching a little.

'I should hope not!' he retorted with mock shock. 'If we had more time I'd do an even better job, but I'm not really dressed for it. Or should I say—*un*dressed? We'll save that for another time. Come on.' He held out the bath sheet as she stood up.

'That was all very therapeutic,' Fay murmured, snuggling into the fleecy folds. 'Where did you learn the technique?'

'Here, and just now. I learned as I went along. Now go and get dressed. Something special. We're going to a ritzy place.'

'You're bossy,' Fay smiled.

He nodded, his mouth a trifle grim. 'When I have to be.'

As Fay came out of the bedroom he was leafing absently through a magazine, frowning. But he stood up quickly, his eyes glinting as they appraised her. The blouse she had chosen shimmered with a soft rainbow glitter above a slim black velvet skirt that defined the slender swell of hips and thighs. As he placed the matching, fingertip-length cape over her shoulders and hooked the black silk frogging at her throat, his fingers dusted her skin briefly, and somewhere under her heart something quivered deliciously.

He had reserved a table at a small, relaxed restaurant where the *chanteuse* was unobtrusive and the atmosphere seemed calculated only to foster a close intimacy. Craig didn't touch her once; there was no swift pressure of his hand across the table, no sudden leaning forward to kiss her lightly, as on previous occasions. She sensed that he was giving her time, easing the pressure, letting her find her own level at her own pace. He talked of unimportant things, and between the courses of *nouvelle cuisine*—which, to Fay's surprise, seemed to stimulate her appetite—she realised that all this was just what she needed.

Only when their coffee was placed in front of them did he say, 'We seem to have a few matters to clear up. Now, what is it you want to know about Claudia and me?'

Fay hesitated, biting her lip and concentrating on stirring her coffee. After a moment, she said, 'You told me that you and Claudia were—simply—friends.'

'We are. What leads you to suspect otherwise?'

'You were somewhere in Cumbria with her recently.' Fay explained about the letter from Vicky.

'Well, that's true enough. Someone Claudia knows is in the process of selling up her house and contents, including some very good paintings. My professional services were required in relation to possible market prices, best means of disposal and so on. Claudia, in fact, put this business my way. I was with Claudia for an hour or so while she introduced me to this acquaintance of hers, and we sat making pleasant conversation over the teacups. The *three* of us.'

'I see,' Fay murmured. 'But there was——' She stopped.

'Go on,' Craig said relentlessly, 'I gather there's more.' His mouth had a hard line.

'Well, some weeks ago you drove Claudia up to Scotland. There was a house party, I understand...' In answer to Craig's surprised expression, she went on, 'Oh, I know about that. Claudia told me when she was over in Paris.'

'Did she?' Craig's voice was terse. 'And I'm being called to account for it, am I? Hasn't what I told you about the Cumbria trip sunk in? There's *nothing* between Claudia and me. And I hope you're not going to make a habit of this kind of enquiry, Fay.'

'If I understood what it was all about, then I wouldn't enquire, would I? It's just that—you didn't even mention Scotland... When I heard about it from Claudia it did seem rather as if you were trying to conceal it. I could only assume that you hadn't wanted me to know about it.'

Under his breath Craig swore. 'Look, let's get one thing straight. Claudia means no more to me than a rather charming acquaintance. I've told you that before, and I expected you to believe me. The Scotland trip wasn't planned. It so happened that I was going up on business at a time when Claudia was going to stay with friends in the same area. Right? And I'm not likely to turn down the opportunity of company on a long car trip. Now, does that answer all your questions?'

Fay hesitated. His anger reached her. If he was as innocent as she now realised, then he had every right to be angry. She nodded.

'And, just for the record,' he added caustically, 'I did try to phone you several times during the last two weeks. There was never any reply.'

'I was working late,' Fay murmured.

'That's what I assumed. I did not immediately jump to the conclusion that you were out on the town with a man,' he said sternly. 'Now, can we drop the subject. I've done enough explaining for one night. This isn't what I came to Paris for,' he said on a note of finality.

Back at the apartment he stood holding her at arm's length. 'Now,' he said softly, 'let's take it from here, shall we?'

She stared up at him. All her suspicions now seemed petty and totally unfounded. How on earth had she managed to get into such a state? She felt as if she had come through a bad dream. Tentatively she put up a finger, touching his lips.

He kissed it. 'You've never been more beautiful,' he whispered.

'That's because you make me—feel beautiful.'

'No more talk,' he said. His hands moved slowly over her face and into the twist of copper hair. She felt him pull out the cut-steel ornament which had secured it, and heard his sudden intake of breath as her hair tumbled down in a curving swathe on to her shoulders. Then, in a sudden spasm of strength which flooded her veins with fire, he lifted her so that her body was pressed closely into his, and her face was level with his own. Still holding her that way, he began to kiss her, his mouth dusting hers with light, almost careless touches, until her lips seemed to throb with longing. After a while he put her down and for a moment stood looking at her. Then he swept her up and carried her into the bedroom.

Her body was quivering as he undressed her slowly, as on that first time, with sensuous, drawn-out torment, so that she both marvelled at and despaired of the self-control he imposed upon himself. What power there was in that strong male body to arouse her so violently! And what strength there was in his will to withhold himself! As his lips travelled over her breasts she gave a little whimper, her head turning from side to side, her body moving ecstatically. She sensed that everything was done with deliberate intent to prolong her pleasure and heighten her sensual responses. Her body craved for the intimacies of his hands, the strong entwining of his legs, the incendiary touch of his tongue. She could only cling to him, her breath torn from her in tiny, beseeching gasps. And, just at the moment when she knew that she couldn't bear any more, he took her with a groan that seemed to rack his very soul. And after that there was only the mounting fervour of a desperate, insatiable hunger for each other.

Then came a vast, dark peace, a hush that seemed almost sacred. Fay touched Craig's damp shoulders, and he held her against himself. She wanted to thank him for the bliss he had brought back into her life.

After a moment he put aside the covers and said, 'Don't go away.'

She laughed. 'Where would I find the energy?'

She sensed his smile in the darkness as he got out of bed and padded out. She heard him moving in the kitchen, opening cupboards and drawers. She heard what sounded like a small explosion, and when he came back she switched on the bedside light to see that he was carrying a tray holding two glasses and the opened champagne bottle.

'Oh, the celebration,' she murmured. 'I'd forgotten.' She put out a hand, but he slapped it lightly.

'Not yet,' he said. Then he sat down on the bed looking at her. 'You look delightfully wanton, half naked...' He lifted the sheet to cover her breasts. 'If I'm not careful I'll get side-tracked.' Then his voice grew serious. 'A while ago I told you that I wanted to marry you. You were careful not to give me an answer. Well, tonight I want one.'

For a moment Fay stared up at him, her eyes huge and limpid. Her heartbeat was a swift, sudden flutter, and it was a second before she could speak.

'But you... I mean, I didn't...'

He frowned. 'Fay, I *told* you. And you heard me. So surely you must have had some thoughts about it?'

She clasped her arms around her knees. 'It's difficult to explain. I was baffled. Yes, you *did* tell me. But—you didn't—ask me. Oh, I know it sounds crazy, but you seemed somehow reluctant. How could I answer when there wasn't a question? I mean, it didn't *sound* like a proposal...'

He gave a hard laugh. 'Then I'm just going to have to convince you, aren't I? What more do I have to say?'

'You could try telling me that—that you love me,' she whispered.

'I've told you repeatedly, but perhaps not in so many words. And I've certainly *shown* you. Very well, if I must spell it out...' He bent and kissed her fiercely. 'Rafaelle Armitage, I love you. With all my heart, I love you. I want to marry you. I want you to say *yes*. And now are you convinced?'

She nodded, her eyes shining, unable to speak.

'So *now*,' he said, on a low, triumphant note, 'we'll celebrate!' He poured the champagne, handed her a glass. 'To us!' he said, with a soft laugh. 'Consider yourself engaged to me. Start thinking of a date and where you'd like to spend a honeymoon.'

'I will,' Fay said docilely. Then she added impishly, 'But do you think this is the right moment for a proposal?'

'Tell me a better one.'

'That's just my point. After making love... Well, come the grey dawn in England things might seem different.'

'Trying to retract, are you? Already?' He laughed. 'Listen. When I first knew that I wanted to marry you I was sitting in a bleak Lincolnshire pub. It couldn't have been greyer. So, you see, my proposal isn't prompted by any post-sexual euphoria, if that's what's bothering you. Stop underselling yourself, Fay. *My* wife will be someone very special indeed.'

CHAPTER NINE

THE hours flew, the weekend passed too quickly. As they sat over their coffee and croissants on Sunday morning, Fay murmured, 'I feel that I want to drag back every moment and hold on to it. But I can't. And it hurts. The minutes slip away, and the hours . . .'

Craig leaned across to silence her with a kiss. 'The best is to come,' he said confidently. 'Soon there'll be no more of these Sunday partings, just a lifetime together.'

'I don't know how you can be so—so sensible and logical,' she complained, laughing. 'I feel—oh, I don't know—all scintillating and fizzy, yet you sit there, coolly drinking coffee and talking good, sturdy common sense to me.'

He took her hand, one long finger stroking each of hers with slow, stirring deliberation, until his movement stopped at the ring they had bought on the previous day. It was a square aquamarine with diamond shoulders. Fay had been bewildered by the choice in the jeweller's and had been unable to make up her mind. 'Try this,' Craig had suggested. 'It's almost the colour of your eyes——' his voice dropped so that the assistant couldn't hear '—when we've made love. Unbelievably clear and beautiful.' Fay had no hesitation after that.

Now he said quietly, 'You just go right ahead feeling scintillating and fizzy—ready for next weekend. *This* weekend is strictly for lotus-eating, but next time we'll get down to business, talk about fixing a date, and so on. I don't know that I can stand much more of this

Channel-hopping. By the way, I can't manage Friday as I'll be tied up, but I'll be here on Saturday.'

'I suppose,' Fay murmured thoughtfully, 'I'll have to think about giving up my job...'

She saw Craig stiffen slightly. 'And you'll hate that, won't you?' he said guardedly.

Fay turned her hand this way and that, watching the light sparkling from her ring. 'Well, I... Yes, in a way. It's been my niche. And I've never seriously considered leaving Paris.' She glanced up, smiling. 'But now, somehow, it doesn't seem too bad.'

'Shall I show you why?' Craig said thickly, standing up. 'Come here...'

Giselle exclaimed in envy when she saw Fay's ring on Monday morning. 'He must be some man,' she breathed. 'Was it love at first sight? You were the very black horse, but I guessed there was a man somewhere. You were strange—one minute up, up, up, and then down. Not like yourself at all. So you will live in Paris? This man—he is a Frenchman?'

'No. Craig's English, and I shall go back to live in England.'

'Ah,' Giselle murmured, nodding, 'to the big house that you own.'

'Yes. I'm going to—to work for myself. I shall still design, of course, but under my own label.'

'And what will your 'usband think of that?' Giselle said, sharpening a pencil meticulously.

Fay laughed. 'It was his suggestion,' she said, 'weeks ago...'

She sat back, staring into space. There would be such a lot to do at Brantye, and it might be a long time before she could put her plan into viable operation. But, as Craig had said, there was a lifetime ahead. 'Don't mention it to anyone else, will you, Giselle?' she said. 'I mean, we haven't actually fixed the date yet. I'll know more after the weekend, then I suppose I'll have to tell Etienne that he'll be needing a replacement. But there's no point in getting him all agitated before it's absolutely necessary.'

She settled down to her work eagerly. The jobs which had seemed dull and boring last week now seemed lively and exciting. How absolutely *right* the world was, she thought, humming happily under her breath.

Even Claudia's telephone call fixing luncheon for the following Thursday couldn't puncture Fay's elation. She seemed to be riding on an exhilarating wind, the days full of movement, colour, event. More, she mused, smiling secretly, in line with Vicky's kind of life. Love must be the greatest catalyst of all, she concluded, as she hurried towards the rue de Rivoli where she had agreed to meet Claudia. Superstitiously she touched her ring; it was her amulet against whatever slings and arrows Claudia might throw at her.

'Just *crudités* and Vichy water for me,' Claudia decided, as they settled into a small booth in the little brasserie. 'You're lucky, Fay. You never had to watch what you eat.' She looked around brightly. 'Now, isn't this nice?' Disarmingly she smiled. Obviously she was determined that this would be a pleasant occasion, Fay thought wryly. Presumably Claudia was hoping that the atmosphere would influence Fay's generosity when Brantye was sold. She's not going to like it one little bit when I tell her that I'm not planning to put the house on the market now, Fay thought, as she cut into her omelette.

It was then that Claudia noticed the ring. 'My goodness, Fay,' she laughed, 'you *are* a dark horse! So secretive... I had no idea! You never gave even the tiniest hint the last time I saw you.'

Fay smiled. 'It's a fairly recent development,' she murmured.

'Do I get to meet this fiancé so that I can congratulate him? Tell me, what's he like? Dark, gallic, irresistible?'

'Dark and irresistible, certainly.' Fay laughed back at Claudia's animated face. 'But not gallic. And you already know him, Claudia,' she added mysteriously.

'Do I?' Claudia frowned. 'I'm totally in the dark,' she said thoughtfully. Her mouth tightened slightly and she took a sip of her wine, then said softly, 'You're not trying to tell me that it's—Craig!'

Fay nodded, her eyes shining. 'You seem rather surprised.'

'Surprised? I'm astounded!' Claudia helped herself to more tomato salad, carefully arranging the rosy slices on her plate as if the design were all-important. Then she looked up at Fay, her eyes bright and sharp. 'You're a fool, Fay. I did warn you. Having a little fling with Craig when he's over here on business is one thing. Taking him seriously is quite another.'

'Oh, but he *intended* me to take him seriously,' Fay said sunnily, watching the light dance on her ring and remembering Craig's voice in her ear, his arms around her.

Claudia dabbed her mouth with her napkin. When she spoke her voice was bland. 'Well, perhaps he did, at that. But no doubt he had his reasons.'

'Yes, he did. The usual ones,' Fay returned placidly.

'You're sure of that?' The thin veneer of friendliness had worn off now, and Fay was reminded of the disharmony of the old days.

'What exactly is that supposed to mean?' she said quietly.

'Can't you guess? Figure it out for yourself.' Claudia's tone was sharp-edged.

'I *am* trying. Perhaps you would give me a clue. Quite honestly, I can't see what you're getting at.'

'Well, then,' Claudia said on a note of low triumph, 'try Brantye for a clue.'

Fay stared at her uncomprehendingly. 'What on earth has Brantye to do with it?'

'At an informed guess—everything.' Claudia paused. 'Well, don't you see? He loves the old place. Exactly as it his, with all his furniture in it. I've sometimes teased him about creating a shrine to Julius.'

Fay began to laugh. 'I'm beginning to see… And that's why he wants to marry me—just to get his hands on Brantye? Oh, Claudia, I've always known that you didn't like me, but this time you've really gone too far! The idea's ridiculous!'

'Is it?' Claudia said, a creamy, catlike smile spreading her lovely mouth. 'I don't think you'd say that if you knew Craig as well as I do.'

Fay's smile faltered as an ice-cold drop formed in her stomach. 'And I can see that you're dying to enlighten me. All right; how well *do* you know Craig?'

'A lot better than you, my dear, if you think that he's marrying you for love!' Claudia said crisply.

Fay put down her fork. 'Don't try to spoil things for me,' she snapped. 'You've done it before, but this time you haven't a chance.'

Claudia shrugged elegantly and changed her tack. 'I must say, you surprise me. You've always had your feet planted firmly on the ground, known exactly where you were going… Well, you may be an intelligent girl; you may be holding down a high-flying job. But when it comes to men, I'd suggest you're naïve.' She paused for a moment, then went on, 'Craig and I have been seeing quite a lot of each other in England. Has he told you that?'

Fay nodded. 'I know that you were with him in Cumbria for business reasons——'

Claudia's laughter tinkled softly. 'The word *business* can cover such a lot, can't it? I don't suppose he told you that I was living at The Lodge for a while, though?'

With a plunging heart Fay recalled the night when Claudia had answered the telephone at Craig's house. She hadn't mentioned that particular incident to Craig; it hadn't seemed important to bring it up last Friday over coffee in the restaurant, as Craig had already convinced her that he and Claudia were merely friends. He had been angry that his relationship with Claudia was ever in doubt, so Fay hadn't pressed the matter.

'I can see that he didn't,' Claudia resumed. 'Well, of course, that's understandable. If he's hell-bent on getting a foothold in Brantye—which obviously he can't afford to buy—then he's not likely to ruin his chances by telling you the *whole* truth, is he?'

'Which is?' Fay's voice was little more than a breath through cold, rigid lips.

'Simply that Craig and I have—something going for us.'

'I—see,' Fay whispered. 'So Craig really loves you, but he's asked me to marry him because he also loves Brantye.'

'That's about the size of it.' Claudia nodded. 'And I must say, Fay,' she added pointedly, 'that, in Brantye, you would be giving him the one wedding present that he really wants.'

Fay stared at her for a long moment. 'You're crazy,' she said dully at last. 'I will *not* believe——'

Again, the sinuous shrug. 'Suit yourself, my dear. But if I were you, I'd think over what I've said. I could be saving you a great deal of heartache. Remember, I was at Brantye after Julius's funeral. I saw the look in Craig's eyes after he heard that the house had been left to you.'

'So he's—engineered a relationship simply to get his hands on the place.'

'The word *simply* doesn't come into it. You know Craig's passion for conservation, preserving old buildings and so on, but I don't suppose you've seen him in action when he's *really* on to something. At least,' she added significantly, 'not until now.'

Fay stood up, tossing down her napkin. 'I absolutely refuse to listen to any more.'

'Just as you wish,' Claudia murmured indifferently. 'But when your little love-nest falls apart, don't say I didn't warn you. Not that Craig won't put on a convincing act; I'm sure he will. With so much at stake a single-minded man can be very devious. However, I can understand your not wanting to believe me, so let's put it to the test and see who's right, shall we?'

Desperately Fay wanted to leave. Claudia's words had sickened her. Yet she felt compelled to stay just so that she would find a flaw in Claudia's argument.

'Yes, let's,' she said brusquely, sinking down on to her chair again.

Claudia drained her glass and said slowly, 'After Craig went off on that lecture tour I was sunning myself in The Lodge garden when a man called—quite a wealthy man, judging from the chauffeur-driven Rolls parked at the gate. It seemed that he was very interested in the future of Brantye. Naturally, I told him that it belonged to my stepdaughter and that it would be going up for sale some time. He was quite persistent with his questions—it turned out that he was a property developer and obviously wanted to be in on the ground floor. So

I referred him to the solicitor, Mr Seymour. And the Rolls purred off in the direction of Mr Seymour's office.'

'I don't see what this has to do with Craig,' Fay objected.

'I haven't finished,' Claudia reproved softly. 'Craig came back from his tour last Thursday, and I told him that someone was sniffing around Brantye. Now, tell me, Fay, just *when* did Craig put that ring on your finger?'

Two days later! a tortured voice screamed in Fay's head. She swallowed an enormous lump in her throat and picked up her handbag. 'You'll excuse me, Claudia,' she whispered, 'I have to get back to work——'

'Of course.' Claudia smiled. 'I was right, wasn't I? Well, whatever you decide to do, good luck, my dear!'

Outside, the bright sunshine stabbed unmercifully as if it intended spotlighting her misery, and for a few moments Fay stood uncertainly outside the brasserie, unclear about what to do next. Then a cruising taxi appeared and she hailed it, giving the driver the address of her apartment. She seemed to be in a kind of limbo, not seeing or hearing the traffic, not even aware of the direction they took. She didn't even hear the echoes of Claudia's words reverberating through her brain. It was as if, somewhere inside her, there had been a cut-off. All she saw was Claudia's coral lips, moving like a character in a silent film.

Back in her apartment she walked around the living-room, idly picking up things—cushions, vases, the clock—and putting them back in place again. It was only when she moved the clock the second time that she realised that she should be back at her desk. Blindly she crossed to the telephone and called Giselle, explaining that something had come up and that she wouldn't be back at the office that day.

'Well, don't worry about that,' Giselle said gaily. 'After all, the company owes you quite a few hours after all the work you've put in.'

Giselle's voice had broken the shell of silence that had insulated Fay from the horrors of lunch.

In the kitchen she made a pot of tea, poured herself a cup with hands that were steady, then, with wry, pursed lips, she sat sipping it without tasting it. She was beyond tears; her heart felt like a dry, hard stone, a painful weight in her chest. I've got to think this through, she kept telling herself, coldly and sensibly. This time I will think with my head and not my heart.

Firstly, Claudia's words seemed to bear out Fay's own theory that Craig had resented her ownership of Brantye, even though he had denied it. Secondly, that odd, bitten-out mention of marriage some weeks ago... A reluctant proposal: reluctant because...? Fay frowned, trying to marshal her thoughts. Reluctant because there was a shred of conscience in even the most hardened criminal? And, heaven knew, Craig wasn't that whatever else he was. So had he felt conscience-stricken over his scheming? Had he, for a moment, been repelled by his own motives? Could that account for his manner on that evening? Wearily Fay raked her fingers through her hair.

But thirdly, had Claudia's news of the developer's interest in Brantye brought him hot-footing it to Paris to put a firm basis under the wedding plans that had, until then, been vague and inconclusive? Was he working against the clock now, pitched into urgency because he could see Brantye slipping out of his hands?

Restlessly Fay got up and went into the bathroom. With cold, resolute hands she undressed and showered, then lay down on her bed. This whole afternoon had a sense of unreality about it.

In spite of her intentions to be objective and analytical, thoughts of her closest moments with Craig intruded, and she shivered as the memory of his ardour possessed her. She recalled tender words, laughter—soft and conspiratorial in the darkness—the incandescent passion they had shared, meals eaten together... It couldn't *all* be an illusion. Could it? Was Craig's professed love for her just one big fake? How desperately he must want Brantye to have put on such a convincing show!

Now other thoughts surfaced in Fay's mind: Craig's early suggestion that she might return to the old house; his persistent unwillingness to accept her decision to sell it. And then, last Friday, his anger at learning that Fay knew of his trips with Claudia! Of course he'd been angry—fearing that it would jeopardise the success of his plans! But he had been able to give a plausible explanation of those outings with Claudia, and Fay had been only too relieved to be reassured, and to believe that *she* was the one he loved. *Because that was what he wanted her to believe!*

Long after the dusk had thickened and the sky was lightened by the diffused glow of floodlit buildings, Fay stared dry-eyed at the ceiling, torn apart by the clamour of silent argument.

Her torment was interrupted by the telephone. Listlessly she got up to answer it.

Christophe's voice seemed to come from another earlier age, and it was a moment before Fay managed to pull herself together and return his greeting in a normal voice.

'I'm asking a favour of you,' he said, 'for——'

'Old times' sake?' Fay murmured, her voice sounding strange in the silent apartment.

'Yes, exactly. I have been let down by my partner for a rather important dinner party tomorrow night.'

Fay bit down an urge to laugh. Christophe, with his obsession with propriety, was probably considering his hostess's feelings at having her numbers and seating arrangements disrupted. Oh, lucky Christophe, Fay thought, if that's all that's on your mind!

'And you'd like me to be your partner?' she prompted.

'I knew you would understand. After all, we are old friends.'

'Yes.' Well, perhaps this was the beginning of a new life which didn't include Craig. 'Thank you, Christophe. I'll look forward to it.'

'It will be rather formal——'

'Don't worry,' Fay said, 'I won't let you down.'

Now why on earth did I agree? she asked herself after he rang off. And yet, she owed Christophe some consideration, even if only for old times' sake. 'Just imagine,' she told her pale reflection in the mirror, 'if you hadn't inherited Brantye you might now be wearing Christophe's ring, unaware that there was a different kind of love—a wild, beautiful, riotous emotion that swept you into heaven.'

And hell. Yes, that, too. Like now.

Back on the bed she stared unseeingly at the window, a lighter rectangle against the darkness, trying to contemplate a future of living with a man she might never completely trust. What kind of basis for marriage was that, for heaven's sake? And what kind of person would she be to condone it?

At last, exhausted, she fell into a light, troubled sleep, waking the following day heavy-eyed and lethargic, remembering with dismay that she had agreed to see Christophe tonight.

That evening she dressed resignedly. One thing in its favour: it would be a temporary escape from the black thoughts which had hovered at the edge of her mind all day, waiting to move in on her whenever she wasn't fully occupied. And she wouldn't have to sparkle for Christophe; that was one consolation. All she had to do was—simply be there.

As she buttoned the long, tight sleeves of the filmy blue dress she thought of the following day—Saturday, when Craig would come, ready to make plans for their wedding. She knew an instant's panic. Should she ask him outright about his motives in wanting to marry her? Hope, pray, that he could reassure her? And if he did, would she be able to believe him? Or would his face betray, for one annihilating second, that there *was* some substance in Claudia's warning?

I won't think about tomorrow, she decided, setting her chin in a resolute tilt. Dear old Christophe deserves more than the company of a woman obsessed by thoughts of another man.

After the rather dull dinner party, driving home in Christophe's opulent car Fay dreaded the loneliness of her apartment and the misery that was waiting to possess her in the night's silence.

'Come up for a nightcap,' she suggested, as they turned the corner. Then she stopped, gripped by an agonising paralysis. There was no mistaking the long, rakish lines, the vertical chrome radiator grille of Craig's parked car. Nor the shadowed face behind the wheel.

'Thank you,' Christophe was saying, 'I will. I won't stay long. Tomorrow I must——'

Fay didn't hear the rest. She was only half aware of getting out of the car, of Christophe locking it. His words were drowned in the loud, frenzied beat of her heart.

With a glance in Craig's direction compounded of uncertainty, appeal and bravado, she hesitated for a second, made an uncertain step towards Craig, then turned and joined Christophe. The expression on Craig's face alarmed and repelled her.

Then even the thunder of her heart was swamped by the surge of power as Craig accelerated away, his tyres screaming.

Fay had the impotent feeling that there was nothing she could do; events had overtaken her. She forced herself into social pleasantries for the next half-hour, but she was relieved when Christophe rose to go.

He didn't seem to have noticed that anything was wrong. Obviously Fay's preoccupation hadn't been obvious. I must be as good an actor as Craig appears to be, she thought bitterly, as she undressed for bed.

CHAPTER TEN

CRAIG arrived early the following morning as Fay was desultorily squeezing orange juice and making toast which she sensed her stomach would reject anyway, but it had seemed important to keep her hands busy. She had not known whether or not she should expect him. His expression the previous night had made her quail, and as she swallowed nervously, staring up at him, she recognised that his mood was unchanged.

A shrivelling chill emanated from him as he filled the doorway, seeming taller and stronger than ever. His features looked as if they had been hewn from rock, his eyes were narrowed to an accusing black glitter as he met her gaze.

But better that he should arrive in this mood, Fay thought, steeling herself, than that he should come with a smile and a sheaf of flowers which would only throw her.

'Now don't pretend that you didn't see me last night,' he snapped, without preamble, closing the door behind him with a deliberate quietness which seemed somehow ominous.

'Of course I saw you. Why should I pretend otherwise?' she retorted. 'But I wasn't expecting you until later today.' Far better if you hadn't come at all, she thought, feeling totally unequal to the occasion.

'That much was obvious!'

Fay shrugged coldly, but inside she was quaking. 'Just in case you've forgotten, you did say that you'd be here on Saturday. Today.'

'The meeting I had arranged for yesterday had to be cancelled. I tried to phone you,' he clipped out. 'For some obscure reason,' he went on sarcastically, 'I was under the impression that you would be pleased to see me a day early, that you would be here and——'

The bitter misery of the last days erupted in an explosion that was almost a relief. 'Yes!' Fay snapped. 'I can imagine! Who can blame you for thinking that? That's the way it's been—you walk into my life and take it for granted that I'll always be here, that my door is always open to you.'

'Hold on a minute!' His dark brows flew together in a threatening black bar. 'Is that so strange? We *are* engaged to be married, you know,' he rasped.

'Correction. We *were* engaged to be married!' The words seemed to come of their own volition, but even as Fay heard them she realised that, subconsciously, the decision had been made on Thursday after she'd left Claudia. She simply hadn't had the courage to voice it before, even to herself. 'I've been a fool,' she went on. 'It's all been so easy for you, hasn't it? I was so gullible——' She stopped, biting off a rising sob. 'But not any more. I've come to my senses now, and I'm seeing things more clearly.'

He reached for her, his hand encircling her wrist with a savagery that made her gasp. 'Just what is that supposed to mean?' he hissed through tight lips.

'I'm sure you don't need me to explain it!' With a sudden jerk of her arm she freed her wrist and went over to the small table. She had to act quickly, decisively, before despair and longing overtook her. From a drawer she picked up the little leather box containing her engagement ring. 'I was mistaken. I think that says it all. But thankfully it's not too late to put things right and——'

'Now wait a minute!' Craig's eyes snapped black fire as he came towards her. Roughly he jerked up her face. 'Before you go off at a tangent—and at a guess I'd say you're over-reacting—don't you think an explanation's in order? First, who was the man you were with last night? The guy who bought you red roses? Christophe?'

'What if it was?' Fay asked coldly, forcing herself to meet his gaze unflinchingly.

Craig's thick lashes seemed to tangle, slitting his eyes and extinguishing their glitter, so that for a moment his face seemed curiously lifeless. 'I see.' The words were two drops of acid, burning her. 'So that's the way the land lies, is it? I seem to have made my share of mistakes, too; I was under the impression that it was all over between you and Christophe. But apparently you're not going to let our engagement cramp your style. Is that how you look at it? I'm just a weekend man, am I? But apparently that's not enough for you.' His tone flayed her.

'It wasn't like that at all! And don't try turning the tables on me, Craig. Don't try putting *me* in the wrong! All you ever wanted was Brantye—I was too blind to see it at the time. But now I——'

'What?' he shouted, glaring at her, his whole body tensed with fury. 'What the hell's got into you? You sound delirious! What on earth's Brantye got to do with *us*?'

'Oh, stop pretending,' Fay said doggedly. 'There's no point, any more. Brantye is all you *ever* wanted——'

'Well, of all the cock-eyed, convoluted . . . So this is how you want to play it, is it? You can blithely ignore the fact that we're going to be married, you can invite men up to your apartment behind my back . . . Except it *wasn't* behind my back last night, was it? Then, when you're caught out, you hand me some garbled line about

Brantye. I do believe that you're accusing me of mercenary motives!' He gave a short bark of laughter. 'Utterly crazy! But it seems that you believe the best method of defence to be attack.'

'I have no need to defend myself,' Fay returned hotly, her eyes like emeralds.

'No? Oh, you mean that, in your book, it's perfectly all right for you to play around while you're engaged to me? That's the way they do things in Paris, is it? Maybe that's why you like Paris so much——'

'And now,' Fay said caustically, 'you're being utterly childish.'

'Strange you should say that, because I was just about to tell you to grow up! What kind of a man do you think you're marrying, for heaven's sake?'

'I'm *not* marrying you,' Fay persisted. 'And *I* don't know what kind of man you are. That's the whole point! I thought I knew you, but I was wrong. And now I don't suppose I'll ever know. Here's your ring. Take it. It would never work.'

She thrust the little box at him, her fingers touching his palm for a single, scalding second. She had the disorientated feeling that this couldn't really be happening: the two of them facing each other like enemies in the sunlit room, the air crackling with violence. But he hadn't denied that Brantye was important to him. Instead, he had stormed in, making it abundantly clear that *he* didn't trust *her*!

He looked down at the little box, tossed it a few inches into the air and caught it deftly. 'Is that your last word?' he gritted.

'Yes, it is. What chance does a marriage have if it's for the wrong reasons in the first place?'

For a moment the smouldering fury in his face seemed to ignite. Then, with obvious self-control, he dropped the ring carelessly into his pocket.

'Well, if that's the way you want it, so be it.'

For a little while the room seemed to throb with the atmosphere of anger and despair.

A cold, lifeless smile flickered across his lips for a moment. 'You don't *really* think *I* fooled *you*, do you? That's so laughable that I'm not even going to sink to the indignity of trying to defend myself. But one thing's sure: you certainly had *me* fooled, Fay. Does that give you any satisfaction? No, don't bother to answer. It doesn't matter now. And anyway, post-mortems can be so boring. So it's goodbye, is it? Well, perhaps in the circumstances we'd better not kiss. We might burn holes in each other's mouths.'

He had regained his self-possession now, Fay saw, and the blistering tone of his voice brought her blood storming into her face. But she compressed her lips and said carelessly, 'Goodbye, then.'

His black gaze swept her figure once. For a second he hesitated, and then he was gone.

The relief of his departure was overwhelming. Fay drew a deep breath and realised that she was trembling violently. Even so, she had to resist the urge to go to the window to watch him leave the building in the faint hope that he might look up, wave, come back, reassure her and put everything right. She laughed shakily. But he wouldn't. He couldn't. She was clear on that point, wasn't she? So why watch the final exit? Why turn the knife? And why even regret the end of a love-affair, so false and mercenary that it could never have survived?

And wasn't it ironic, she asked herself, that Christophe—the man who never for one moment had threatened her emotions—should have featured at the very end of such a crazy, wonderful, heartbreaking chapter of her life? The odd, broken noise in her ears was, she realised after a moment, the sound of her sobs.

Two hours later, with a sensation of having been dragged through a millrace, Fay sat down with pen and paper. Focusing red, swollen eyes, she wrote to Mr Seymour asking him to make the necessary arrangements for the sale of Brantye. That lovely, revelationary chapter of her life was over. Dead. Fool's gold.

What she must do now was turn right around and get herself going again.

During the following weeks she applied herself to her work with a single-mindedness that surprised even Giselle, who had the sensitivity not to remark on the coincidence of Fay's frenzied energy and the absence of the ring from her finger.

Occasionally, in the evening, Fay made up a foursome with Giselle and Arnaud and his friend, Victoire. Fay would chat gaily, dance feverishly, enthuse madly until even Giselle grumbled about the pace she set. But inside herself Fay knew a desperation that would not allow her to slow down lest the black abyss of pain enveloped her. What had Craig done when he left her apartment? Gone straight back to England and Claudia? Had Claudia been able to comfort him?

Fay's mind skittered away. To lose herself in the present was the only way of dealing with the past, and her main concern was to put as much event and activity between the here-and-now and that sunny Saturday morning when Craig had walked out of her life for good.

And, gradually, Fay's old lifestyle began to build its pattern again, punctuated by a business trip to Rome and occasional dates which always seemed vaguely unsatisfactory, but helped to get her through the evenings.

Vicky telephoned to say that the play had folded and that she was now back in London doing some promotional work in a trade exhibition. A letter from Mr Seymour stated that he had received an offer for Brantye, and that there was a further box of family effects which Fay might be interested in collecting some time.

Fay had just returned to Paris from an exhausting trip to New York and was wearily unpacking her suitcase when the phone rang. For a moment she thought of ignoring it. All she wanted to do was sleep. But the ringing persisted, and when she answered it she couldn't place the voice until the caller identified himself as Nick, the boy who occupied the flat next to Vicky's.

He sounded distraught. 'Vicky's broken her leg,' he explained quickly. 'She'll kill me for ringing you, but I looked up your number when I was in her place trying to fix her a meal, and——'

'I'll come,' Fay said instantly. 'I'll be over tomorrow.'

'Oh, great.' His relief was evident. 'I've been trying to get hold of you for the past three days. I was getting desperate because I have to go away myself...'

'Don't worry about that. And thank you for letting me know. I'll take care of everything.'

'But don't tell her I called you. Invent some excuse if you can.'

'I've got some business to see to in England, anyway. I'll make that my reason for coming...'

Wearily Fay began to pack her case again. She would have to go in to work tomorrow and see Etienne to give her report on the trip. Jeanne, the merchandiser who had accompanied her, would be able to fill in the details... And then—England. And Sussex... Her stomach churned coldly.

When Vicky's leg is better I'll take her on a cruise with some of the money from the house sale, Fay decided, resolutely turning her thoughts away from perilous channels. I shall be quite wealthy, I suppose. I'll need some advice about investing the money.

She sat down suddenly. She ought to feel happy about future security, she realised, but somehow it didn't seem to count for very much.

And there was Claudia... Claudia—whose words had ruined everything between Fay and Craig. Or had they? Perhaps Claudia had averted what would, ultimately, have been a tragedy. One more statistic in the broken marriages file. Fay sighed. She would make Claudia a gift; after all, years ago Claudia had been able to snap Fay's father out of his grief. That had to be worth a lot in spite of later events. Fay shook her head, forcing her mind on to other matters.

It was with a sense of relief that Fay opened the door of Vicky's flat the following evening. Here, at least, she was at ease, and Vicky's surprised welcome warmed her heart, although her sister's shrewd comments on Fay's appearance were unflattering.

'Put it down to jet lag,' Fay retorted lightly. 'I've only just come back from New York, and the pace was frantic, but I thought I'd better attend to my business with Mr Seymour, so here I am. And what do I find? You—like this!'

'Just rotten luck,' Vicky said. 'Still, it was a simple break. I was tripping lightly down the stairs at the exhibition hall, and that's exactly what I *did*—tripped. *Not* the most graceful exit I've ever made!' She patted the plaster cast. 'I'll be glad to get this chunk of hardware off my leg.'

'I was thinking... When you can get about again, we might go off on holiday,' Fay suggested, plumping up one of the cushions behind Vicky's head, and pulling a small table close to her chair. 'A cruise, perhaps?'

'Can't afford it,' Vicky grimaced. 'I'm husbanding my resources. Who knows when I might get work again?'

'My treat,' Fay assured her, pouring tea and handing Vicky a cup. 'I've had an offer for Brantye which Mr Seymour recommends I accept. I'm going over to his office on Friday to sign some papers and collect a box of Father's things—old rowing trophies and so forth.'

She was pierced by a sudden vision of Brantye, and of Craig discovering the tarnished trophies at the back of a cupboard somewhere...

Friday came, a day of promise with a clear blue sky and sunshine, a perfect early July day. But Fay felt chilled and apprehensive as she drove out of London and joined the broad dual carriageway south, concentrating on maintaining her place in the fast traffic. She wished that she were wearing something warmer than the light blue shirtwaister.

At the solicitor's office she was told by his secretary that Mr Seymour had been unexpectedly called out but would be back in an hour or so. 'In the meantime,' the young woman suggested, 'perhaps you would like to drive over to the house and pick up the box of effects.'

'Oh... Yes, of course.' For some reason Fay had assumed that her father's things would be here. A rather silly idea, she realised now. And she knew that, at the root of it, lay her unwillingness to see Brantye again. However, there was nothing she could do except act on the woman's suggestion.

A strange lassitude seemed to engulf her. This was where it had all begun on that April day when she had learned of her inheritance over an uncomfortable lunch. Now she wanted nothing more than to pick up the box, sign the papers and head back to London. Her connection with this part of Sussex would then be completely broken.

As she drove through the leafy lanes she resolutely shut her mind to the memories which they evoked. As she passed through the gates of Brantye and drove by The Lodge she stared straight ahead. But from the corner of her eye she noticed that there was no sign of Craig's car, and she felt a slight slackening of her tension. Of course, he travelled around a lot, and it was unlikely that he would be here at this time of day.

This will take no longer than a minute, she urged herself. Then she would return the keys, wait for Mr Seymour, and hopefully be back with Vicky well before teatime. Everything nicely tied up apart from the actual completion of the sale contract. And that could be dealt with by post.

She ran up the shallow steps and put the key in the lock. But, as before, the door swung inward. Awareness shivered along her spine, and she froze. 'Who's there?' she called sharply, then winced as she saw that the hall was exactly as it had been the last time she was here. Unable to stop herself, she lifted her head to look up at the gallery.

She seemed to have been caught in a time warp. That shiver of awareness should have warned her... Craig opened the door of one of the upper rooms—the same door through which he had first appeared on that never-to-be-forgotten afternoon.

On legs that had lost their strength Fay swayed towards the big monk's bench by the wall and sat down. The blood seemed to have drained out of her heart, leaving it painfully constricted. Unable to look away, she watched Craig come slowly down the stairs, his gaze never leaving her face.

Fay was stricken by a wild urge to run out, drive away—anywhere... Anywhere that could provide a refuge from the sight of him. But she was unable to move. She was held as securely as if she were part of the bench.

'Well, well,' Craig said softly, as he reached the foot of the stairs. His voice sparked off a flame inside her, and she had a devastating flashback to the days and nights when his lips had teased her ear with whispered endearments.

She drew a ragged breath. Could she have forgotten how virile he looked, how powerfully attractive he was? He was in a black T-shirt and oatmeal-coloured trousers, and his impact hit her afresh, cancelling her efforts at getting herself together over the past weeks. But there was no smile—only a hard, neutral mask, a tough, beautifully muscled body standing in front of her.

Fay found her voice at last, hearing her brittle tones as if they came from someone else. 'Well, well, indeed! This is a surprise. I didn't expect to find *you* here.'

'Or you wouldn't have come,' Craig supplied.

No, I wouldn't, Fay cried silently. Fear would have kept me away, fear of the feelings I'm experiencing at this moment: love and longing, and the bitter knowledge that I never got over loving you. I never will.

But, out of a well-schooled strength born of the adversity of earlier years, she managed an indifferent shrug. 'I won't ask what you're doing here, but——' she looked around, her brows lifted '—you really must get your things out. I'm surprised that Mr Seymour hasn't had something to say about that. The house is as good as sold, I understand.' Knowing how Craig felt about the place, and even bearing in mind his mercenary motives, and his deception, she couldn't watch his face. 'I've simply come to collect some more of my father's things.'

Craig nodded. 'They're in the library. The box contains some old school reports—some of yours. And there's a delightful photograph of Vicky as a baby and——'

'Thank you,' Fay cut in. 'You needn't go into details. I'll look through them when I get back to London.'

There was a sudden thick silence when the walls of the house seemed to close in upon her, suffocating and stifling. Making a supreme effort, she stood up.

'How is Vicky?' Craig asked laconically.

'Fine... That is, apart from a broken leg.'

'I'm sorry to hear it. So that's why you're over here, is it?'

'That's the main reason.' Fay faced him brightly. 'I'm looking after her for a little while. I remember you once accused me, more or less, of not caring about her. You were wrong, you see.'

'So it would seem, but we all make mistakes.'

Yes, Fay thought, hardening her heart against the effect of his nearness.

'And Claudia?' he asked. 'Do you hear from her?'

Fay swallowed. 'Why should I?' she asked in a composed voice. 'I've no idea where she is, but I assumed that she was here in England.'

'Oh, no.' Craig shook his head, smiling faintly. 'You're miles out. She's in the Bahamas.'

'Oh, well, naturally you would know more about her movements than I.' Absently she picked up a tiny ivory figure from a table and focused her attention on the delicate carving. How strange that even during this agonisingly difficult conversation Claudia's name should crop up.

Craig made an indifferent gesture. 'And how's Christophe?'

Fay put the figure down firmly, dusting off her hands. 'I've no idea,' she replied briskly. 'The last time I saw him was on that Friday evening when you saw us and——'

'Jumped to the wrong conclusions? Is that what you were going to say? Fay——' he took a step towards her '—it could be that we *both* jumped to the wrong conclusions.'

Fay looked away from him quickly. His words had made her heart leap with hope, but resolutely she mastered herself. He's still trying, a voice in her head warned her. He still thinks it might not be too late to get his hands on Brantye. 'Oh, I don't think so,' she said coolly at last. But in spite of her words her heart seemed to be following a different tack. It was slow torture even being in the same room with him. His whole figure, the sudden light in his eyes, the very presence of the man, pulled her like a magnet. She moved away towards the library. 'Incidentally, do you know this—this property developer who's buying the house?' she said. Not that she was the slightest bit interested, but she simply must escape the treachery of her own yearnings and keep her thoughts on a mundane plane.

'Property developer?' Craig frowned, then his face cleared. 'Oh, yes, there *was* a developer interested in Brantye. But I made a better offer. Your bank balance looks like being very healthy indeed,' he added sardonically.

Fay stared, then sank down into a chair. 'I don't think I heard... You mean, *you're*——'

'Buying the house?' Craig finished as her voice died. 'Yes, that's what I said.' He studied her, a grim smile playing across his mouth.

Fay's face burned in the flames of mortification that seared her. Her heartbeat was so rapid that she could hardly breathe and the blood pounding her temples blurred her vision. In wordless realisation she stared at him for a few moments, then got up and moved blindly to the window to lean her forehead against the cold glass. It was almost two minutes—two minutes of forcing herself to see the hideousness of her mistake—before she turned round, tears glistening on her lashes. 'So I was wrong,' she said dully. 'What can I say?' She dragged in a deep breath, trying to arrange her thoughts. 'But knowing how you loved this house, and how you feel about certain things being lost—and—heritage—and... I'm sorry,' she murmured incoherently.

Craig was still standing in the same place, his hands thrust deep into his pockets. He watched her closely as if trying to see behind the façade into the very heart of her. She couldn't bear his scrutiny; she didn't want to know what he thought of her. Not again. 'So what will you do with the house?' she said vaguely. 'Live in it?'

He shrugged. His eyes were wintry and his mouth had a sombre twist as he said, 'No, it's far too big for me. I simply wanted to preserve it. There must be some good use it can be put to, and so long as I own it I shall be able to have some say in things. I would have loathed seeing those old trees felled to make way for an expensive housing estate. And there's Julius's wild garden—at least that will be safe from the bulldozers.'

Fay nodded. 'I know how important that is to you.' She lifted her hands helplessly. 'That's why it all seemed to make sense when I'd had time to think over what Claudia——' She stopped suddenly. There was no purpose in going over old ground and, besides, the mention of Claudia's name reminded her that Craig hadn't shown much honesty about his affair with her stepmother. 'I'd better go,' she jerked out. 'I don't like leaving Vicky cooped up alone for too long...'

But in one lithe step Craig had reached her side. 'Not just yet,' he snapped. His hands were on her shoulders, spinning her round to face him. 'Claudia? What's Claudia got to do with it?'

Fay shut her eyes, turning her head away, afraid of the power which seemed to flow through his hands. She tried unsuccessfully to shrug them off. 'It doesn't matter,' she muttered.

'Oh, but it *does*! It matters very much to me. Don't you think I'm entitled to an explanation, damn it? You made an accusation against me in Paris, remember? And now you're here I'd like to know what grounds you had for it. Understand? I'm sorry, Fay, but you're not leaving here until you tell me.'

She stared up at him, her eyes shadowed with misery. Couldn't he see just what his touch was doing to her? Had he no idea of the sensual power he had over her? She looked away, battling with a driving need to lay her head against the broad chest and tell him how sorry she was. But he wouldn't be interested in her remorse; his opinion of her had reached rock-bottom the night he saw her with Christophe.

'Oh, Craig, let it go,' she whispered wearily at last. 'What does it matter what Claudia said?'

'Are you crazy?' He gave her shoulders a tiny shake, his fingers biting into her flesh. 'Of course it matters!'

'Well... She told me that you and...' Fay shook her head wildly. 'I had trusted you. I believed you when you told me that Claudia was simply a... Oh, what's the use? Why put me through it like this? There's no *point*!'

'I demand to know,' he bit out. '*That's* the point!'

Stiffening her mouth against the silent sobs that tugged at it, Fay whispered, 'Claudia and I lunched together the day before you came to Paris. She saw my ring. She—

alerted me to—to certain matters which I hadn't considered. She——'

'Suggested that all I was interested in was the acquisition of Brantye. Is that it?'

'She said—and somehow I had already got the impression—that you couldn't afford to buy it...'

Craig's hands dropped in sheer surprise, and he gave an incredulous laugh. 'Then let me put at least *one* of you right. I could buy this place three times over, if I wished. And I have a shrewd feeling that Claudia knew that.'

Fay took the opportunity to move away. 'But—I don't understand... If that's the case, why didn't you buy Brantye at the beginning when I told you that I was going to sell it?' She stared at him with wide, baffled eyes, absently rubbing her shoulder where the touch of his fingers still stung.

'For the simple reason that you didn't seem absolutely sure you wanted to sell. There was a reluctance in you to let it go out of your family. I sensed it and, anyway, you admitted it once. I had no desire to influence you in any way. I had to be sure you really wanted to sell the house before I made my move. So I waited.' He gave a crooked, self-mocking smile. 'Another mistake. It gave Claudia time to put some very peculiar ideas into your head, apparently.'

Fay looked down at her hands idly pleating the blue cotton of her skirt. Shame seemed to be engulfing her like a destructive flame. She could hardly believe how wrong she had been. Why, oh, why had she listened to Claudia? Surely she should have seen through her. And yet, Claudia had been so convincing, and there were small, unexplained aspects of Craig's behaviour that Fay's uncertainty had fed upon.

'Damn it, Fay,' Craig growled, 'what I can't stomach is that you believed her! Didn't those days and nights we spent together count for anything at all?'

Fay closed her eyes, shaking her head from side to side. Why did he have to mention those days and nights? Hadn't his explanation made her wretched enough without reminding her of the happiness they had once shared?

'I'm sorry,' she whispered. 'So sorry, but you see——'

'Sorry? I think you should be. Let me get this straight. Presumably Claudia must have told you about this property developer's interest?' When Fay nodded, he went on thoughtfully, 'Yes, I see. So you were led to believe that it forced my hand.'

Fay nodded again dully.

Mercilessly, Craig went on, 'So, with another party interested in the house, I had to act quickly. And, as it seemed that I couldn't afford to buy the place, marrying you was my only option.'

'I . . . Oh, I couldn't think straight,' Fay murmured brokenly. 'You see, I kept remembering things . . . Even when you first spoke of marriage it sounded almost as if you hated the idea . . . Oh, I can't explain.'

Craig raked long fingers through his hair, his expression bewildered. 'Of course I didn't hate the idea. How could I? Marriage was all I wanted. But there was something about you in those days that often held me at arm's length. Something warning me not to rush you. I sensed that, without quite understanding it. And I was angry with myself . . . I *did* rush you, after all. I wanted you so much . . . And I'd already made one mistake—that night at Vicky's party when I asked you back to my place. I tried to avoid making the same mistake again. Too much was at stake.'

'What can I say?' Fay murmured, after a moment. 'It's just that—some of the things Claudia said, and some of the things I remembered and thought about—were like pieces in a jigsaw. I put them together——'

'And *made* them fit!' Craig said bitterly.

'Yes,' Fay said in a low voice, 'as *you* did—about Christophe and me. I stopped seeing him several weeks ago. Then, after Claudia had been——'

'You took up with him again,' Craig said savagely.

'No! I *didn't*. But he'd been let down by a dinner partner and I stood in for her. Nothing more than that. Even if you don't believe me, it's the truth. Anyway,' she went on, almost to herself, 'for one evening it helped me not to think about you.' She stopped, then resumed, 'And there's something I haven't told you. I don't know whether to believe it or not. I just don't seem to be certain of anything any more...'

'Go on,' Craig prompted, but his voice was gentle, and his eyes seemed to understand her reluctance.

'Claudia told me...' Fay swallowed painfully, then pressed her palm against her chin to steady it '...that you and she were—were...'

'Lovers?' Craig prompted softly.

Blindly Fay groped for the arm of the chair and sank down. Thinking about Craig and Claudia had been agony enough, but to be rehashing it like this was infinitely worse. At any moment she would weep. And tears weren't the answer. She had to be strong. She took a deep breath and forced herself to sit erect in the high-backed chair, pressing her spine against the carved fruit and flowers, almost welcoming the physical discomfort. 'Well, Claudia didn't actually say it in so many words. But she conveyed the impression that—you were having a love-affair.' Fay moistened dry lips. 'And she told me that she'd been staying at The Lodge, and that the business trips you'd made with her weren't—weren't purely for business reasons.'

Under his breath Craig swore savagely, his face thunderous. Fay put out an uncertain hand towards him, but he didn't see it. 'And you believed her!' He beat his fist against the palm of his other hand. 'It's true enough that Claudia *did* stay at The Lodge. But not while I was there! Good heavens, Fay, what do you think I am? Some kind of cheap Casanova? Claudia stayed at my place while I was away on that lecture tour. But obviously she didn't tell you *that*!'

For a moment they stared at each other. Craig's face was white with anger, a muscle in his cheek flicking rhythmically. At last Fay's glance fell away. She felt close to collapse.

'I'm—sorry,' she whispered at last. 'I can't tell you how much I... At the time it sounded—plausible...' Her voice trembled into silence as she faced the enormity of what she had lost. And all because she had chosen to believe Claudia rather than Craig.

'So you—weren't in love with her after all?' she breathed.

'Damn it, I've told you often enough,' Craig gritted.

Fay passed a weary hand over her forehead. 'Claudia must have hated me,' she murmured, almost to herself. 'We never really hit it off, and I haven't much respect for her, but... But to have deliberately lied just to ruin our relationship...' She stared into space, shaking her head uncomprehendingly.

'Come on,' Craig said suddenly. 'We both need a drink.' He stretched out his arms and pulled her up. His hands felt strong and safe as they enveloped hers. 'You're shivering, and your hands are like ice.'

He took Fay's arm as he led her out and down the drive to The Lodge, and she leaned against him weakly, still trying to come to terms with the immensity of Claudia's hatred for her.

Dully she saw that Craig's sitting-room was furnished comfortably with bookcases and two cream and coral striped sofas facing each other across a marble-topped coffee-table, but she didn't really take anything in. Her mind seemed stunned, her body inexpressibly weary, and she sank on to one of the sofas gratefully. She wasn't even aware that Craig had left the room until he came back carrying a tray holding two large mugs of coffee. 'I've put a good measure of brandy into yours,' he said. 'You look as if you need it.'

She managed to summon up a wan smile. 'It's been quite a morning,' she murmured, cupping the mug in both hands, grateful for its warmth. 'And then to be faced with the realisation that Claudia must have loathed me for years... Well, it doesn't do much for my self-esteem...' The attempted laugh turned into a sob, and she took a sip of coffee to stifle it.

'You're wrong. Claudia didn't ruin our engagement because she hated you. You mustn't think that.' He put down his mug and stood up, thrusting his hands into his pockets and moving away. He took a book from the shelves, absently leafing through it. 'I didn't intend telling you this, but in the circumstances I must. I can't bear seeing you so—low.' He spoke so quietly that Fay had to strain to catch his words.

'Claudia delivered the kiss of death because she was jealous of you. A few weeks ago I began to realise that she was—shall we say—getting interested in me? Oh,' he gave a harsh laugh, 'perhaps not in me so much as my bank balance.'

'Is this the truth?' Fay whispered. 'You're not just saying this to make me feel less—low?'

'It's the honest truth.' Craig put the book back and came to sit beside Fay. 'Look at me, darling.'

Fay felt a little flame run through her veins. Her body seemed to be coming back to life, warmed by the closeness of him.

'Bank balance?' she murmured. 'But Claudia thought——' Then she stopped.

'That I spent all my money on preserving bits of the countryside? Is that what you were going to say?'

'Well—yes. She seemed to think that—that you didn't have much money.'

'You've got it wrong. She might have said that to *you*, because that's what she wanted you to believe. Don't you see? It substantiated her story that I couldn't afford Brantye. You know,' Craig resumed thoughtfully, 'Claudia could be pleasant company, and she's a lovely woman. But she was never for me. But,' he shrugged, 'she had different ideas. And I suppose it must have been after I told her that you and I had become engaged the previous weekend that she decided to make one more bid. This is all conjecture, of course, and based on what you've told me... But I figure that she fixed up that lunch with you in Paris with the deliberate intention of parting us.'

'And I—I let her succeed,' Fay breathed.

Craig gave Fay's hand a swift, crunching squeeze. 'Of course, I had no idea that she'd been to Paris to see you, that is—not until you told me so today. She came to Brantye the following Tuesday. I suppose my mood and my expression told her that her plan had succeeded.' He gave a short, bitter laugh. 'And that was borne out when she found your engagement ring. I'd tossed it into a corner somewhere. She spotted the box and opened it...'

'Craig...' Tentatively Fay put out a hand. 'Let's not talk about it any more. It's all so—so *ugly*.'

He gave a wry smile. 'There isn't much more to say, anyway. Without going into detail, Claudia made it clear that if I gave her a ring she wouldn't hand it back... When, eventually, she understood that I had absolutely no intention of doing any such thing, there was a brief and rather unpleasant scene. But at least she'd got the message.' He grimaced, then gave a relieved sigh. 'There. I think that's the end of the story so far as Claudia's concerned. Not that there ever *was* much of a story, really.'

'So that's why she's gone to the Bahamas?' Fay said musingly.

It all seemed too much to take in at once... Brantye. And now the love-affair which had existed only in Claudia's desires... Something in Fay's body seemed to sing. Numbed nerves flickered into awareness. Her body seemed to belong to her again; she was even capable of thinking straight. How gullible she'd been, and how utterly wrong! But the coffee and brandy alone couldn't have restored her so miraculously: no, it was the realisation that Craig had never loved Claudia; it was his spontaneous use of the word *darling*...

And he was smiling at her, his eyes warm. 'Yes,' he replied softly, 'that's one reason why Claudia's gone. You recall I told you about her friend in Cumbria who was disposing of some paintings? She was actually selling her home here and going to live abroad. She had offered Claudia the post of companion and secretary.' He paused for a moment. 'I suppose my attitude finally decided Claudia in favour of the idea.'

Fay nodded. 'I see.' She was quiet for a moment, then she said in a low voice, 'We've all been so wrong. You were wrong about Christophe, Claudia was wrong about you, and I... Well, I...' Her voice died, then she said quickly, 'I can only say it again, Craig—I'm so very sorry...'

But even the word seemed inadequate in expressing her regret. How could it possibly cover all the heartache, the betrayal?

She felt the prick of tears and she blinked hard. She mustn't cry now! Save the weeping for later when she was alone.

But Craig had noticed. He drew Fay towards him so that her head lay against his chest. She felt the warm strength of bone and muscle beneath her cheek, breathed the distinctive woodsy-mossy scent that was part of him. Whatever happens now, she thought tiredly, at least we won't part as enemies. 'I'm so pleased that you just happened to be at Brantye this morning,' she murmured. 'I'm grateful for the opportunity to explain and apologise.'

There was little more to be said now, she realised, with a bleak sense of overwhelming loss. Eventually, if Craig ever thought of her at all, it would be as a one-time girlfriend, lover, fiancée who had ended the affair by her own blindness.

She sat up, reaching for her handbag. 'I must go,' she said tonelessly. 'I have to see Mr Seymour and there's Vicky——'

She stopped as Craig's hand covered her own. 'Did you really think that I *just happened* to be at Brantye when you arrived?' he said softly.

'I—well, I... Yes.' She stared at him, her eyes wide, searching his face. 'Was it—more than—just coincidence?' she whispered.

'Very much more. I asked Seymour's secretary to let me know when you were coming.'

'Why?' Fay's question was little louder than a sigh, drowned by the sudden thunder of her heart.

'Several reasons.' His other hand came up to touch her hair wonderingly. 'To start with, I had to see you again. It was a hunger, a disease, a wildness... I couldn't get free of it. And yet I couldn't come to you. Not in Paris. It had to be here because of——'

'Christophe?' she said gently. 'Oh, Craig, compared with you Christophe didn't even begin to...'

'I wasn't sure. You had behaved so strangely that Saturday morning in Paris. And I was so jealous, so resentful that he was there while I was here. I decided to set the stage exactly as it was when you came before, remember? I thought that, if I surprised you, your face might show me what I wanted to see. But it didn't. Not then.'

'And—now?' Fay breathed.

He tilted her chin and looked down into her face, his eyes lit by the intensity of his need. She felt the heightening throb of her blood, the leaping *frisson* in her spine. Then slowly his mouth came down. She gave a little moan, parting her lips softly to receive the sensuous warmth of his answer.

He held her with a tenderness that reached into her heart, then he said quietly, 'You know, darling, even the happiest of marriages hold a fair proportion of mistakes.' She felt his lips caressing her throat. 'We got off to a good start even before we reached the altar,' he added ruefully. 'The important thing is to talk the problems through.'

'Yes, I know,' Fay murmured, her hand moving over his hair. 'But the last time—in Paris—everything got out of hand and——'

'And so quickly. We didn't give ourselves enough time.'

Fay nodded as his lips brushed her eyelids. 'I know. Just a few minutes and—everything was over.'

'But we can make time begin again for us. Years and years of time together, if that's what we want.' He pulled away from her, cupping her face in his hands and looking into her eyes. 'I want it more than anything... How about you?'

And Fay, whose hopes had soared wildly during the last moments, could only gaze back at him, and pluck one word out of the magic of the morning. 'Yes,' she whispered. Then, after a moment, 'Oh, *yes*, my love.'